# MURDER WITH LILIES

## A CHANCE INQUIRY NOVEL

# HOLLY NEWMAN

OLIVER-HEBER BOOKS

Cover art by Dar Albert at Wicked Smart Designs

Gloriosa Superba/Kalihari illustration by Paula Swenson-Sword

Published by Oliver-Heber Books

0 9 8 7 6 5 4 3 2 1

# PROLOGUE

## NOVEMBER 1815. SUMMERWORTH PARK, KENT

"My dearest wife, what are you about?"

James's voice, laced with affectionate laughter, sent the rust-and-black tabby kitten Cecilia had been attempting to befriend scurrying away.

"Now see what you've done?" she said, looking up at him standing in the stable doorway, a dark, back-lit image against the streaming sunlight trying to enter the stable. He looked like one of her Aunt Jessamine's silhouettes. "I have been enticing the creature to come to me for the past fifteen minutes, and she was nearly at my fingertips when you scared her off."

"Her?" He walked toward her, and the dark silhouette resolved into James, clothed in riding attire.

Cecilia shrugged. "Or he, makes no matter." She held out her hand.

James obligingly stepped forward to draw her to her feet.

She brushed the dust and straw from the front of her twilight-blue figured muslin gown. "I thought I should like a cat in the house."

"A cat?"

"Yes. I had one as a young girl, and seeing the barn cat's kittens brought back memories."

James nodded, understanding more than Cecilia would say. While her mother lived, there had been joy in her life. The kitten represented old joyous memories. He believed—hoped—that in the six months they'd been wed he'd brought joy back to her. "Memories of when your mother was alive?"

"Yes," she said shortly. She twisted around to brush off the back of her skirts.

So, it wasn't just memories, he thought, though they might have served as gestation. He pulled a piece of errant straw from her pale blonde hair. "Keep working on her—or him. I don't see how they could resist you. I know I can't," he whispered, as he pulled her into the circle of his arms.

"James! The servants!" she protested half-heartedly as he lowered his head to kiss her, and she put her arms around his neck.

When he broke off the kiss and lifted his head, Cecilia sighed.

He tucked her arm into the crook of his as he led her back to the manor house. He walked slowly, for they were in no hurry. There was no one waiting for them, nothing they needed to be doing. He looked up at the Summerworth Park manor, and beyond as far as he could see, and felt content. He'd purchased the estate last spring from his cousin, Gideon Tallavest, the Earl of Monteith. They had transformed the estate over the last six months they had been in residence. Gone was the shabby old lady, past its prime. In its place, they'd resurrected a welcoming grand dame. Even now, with the leaves and flowers gone to sleep for winter, there was an elegance in the estate.

He and Cecilia had much to be proud of for their efforts over the past six months. They had certainly been busy. But now, with winter's approach, was the quiet time, a time for reflection and planning for the new year. Quiet times did not sit well with his Cecilia.

And that, he knew, was behind the interest in the cat.

"You're feeling restless," he said, as they walked up the stone steps of the terrace to enter the house through the glass doors of the morning parlor, named for the morning sunlight that streamed through its long windows.

He felt her shoulders slump.

"Yes, I suppose I am," she admitted. "With our investigations last spring and all the work on the estate over the summer, it has been a full year. A delightful year," she added.

"The investigations we could have done without. I do not consider you almost getting killed 'delightful,'" he drily observed.

"But James, we would not have met if it weren't for my investigations."

"My love, I think I would have been drawn to you however we met."

She smirked up at him. "So you say now."

"And so I know. We would have met one way or another, and I was drawn to you like a moth to a flame."

"Oh, listen to you! Outrageous! I shall not heed you. But I am restless. Life is too quiet, and that concerns me."

"I trust you are not wishing for another investigation like our spring adventure?"

She looked sideways at him. "We did well," she said.

"By the grace of God!" he declared.

"Nonsense. We are a good team—you must admit that."

"I thought you were considering setting up Mr. Thornbridge in the inquiry agent business?"

"I was, but I am now convinced he shouldn't like that. He wants to leave the city. He is attending lectures and reading all manner of books on land and estate management. His plan now is to be an estate steward."

"That requires more than lectures and book learning," James said.

"I know, but he is determined to make a career change once Waddley's is sold. We will see what we might do to assist him."

"We?"

"Naturally," she said, giving him a sly glance and smile. "As if I would do anything without my wonderful husband."

"Why do I feel, my lady wife, that you are attempting to manipulate me?"

"Me? Such nonsense you speak, James," Cecilia teased.

He laughed, then sobered and patted her hand where it lay across his arm. "Actually, I knew of Thornbridge's plan and had put out the word on his behalf. I may have come across the perfect solution for him that will require his business acumen as well as estate stewardship."

"What is that?"

"One of my cousin's entailed properties enjoys high-quality clay deposits of the kind used for porcelain figurines and tableware. He has it leased to one of the big pottery companies, but he has concerns they are taking more than agreed, and his estate steward only concerns himself with the tenant farms and the home farm, knowing nothing about the business of clay mining. When Gideon looked closer at the books for that property, he saw the potential for a nice profit that will help him pull the earldom out of the River Tick. He needs an estate agent who can negotiate with the pottery company and keep them honest."

Cecilia thought. "That might serve," she said slowly. "Sounds like something he could really get involved in, with lots of learning potential."

"Such was my thought. I owe him a debt of gratitude for his efforts on your behalf."

"James, gratitude doesn't cover it. The man took a knife in his side while seeking information for me!"

"I know, I know."

"The sale doesn't close for another couple of weeks. Now that the terms are agreed upon, the solicitors and the banks have paperwork to draw up. We will need to go to London for the signing."

"As restless as you are, are you certain you don't wish to go sooner? Or perhaps to your grandfather's until then? They are expecting us for Christmas, along with your Aunt Jessamine and her family."

She wrinkled her nose. "No, as much as I love Grandfather, a little of the Duke of Houghton goes a long way. I shall put off that pleasure for a while longer. I know I should relax and enjoy the quiet while I can. In my soul, I am gripped by the feeling it won't last."

# CHAPTER ONE

## LATE NOVEMBER 1815. EAST INDIA DOCKS, LONDON.

"*R*ani! Rani!" The child's plaintive cry pierced the pandemonium of the London wharf.

Rani Rangaswamy spun away from the man she'd approached for directions. She'd left Krishan not twenty feet away, sitting amongst their motley assortment of trunks, boxes, and portmanteaus. *He was gone.*

"Krishan!" she called out, listening in every direction for his voice, searching among the teeming throngs of people and goods for a sight of her charge.

To her right, tall-masted ships from India and the Far East lined the wharf, and to her left, a line of brick warehouses three stories tall nearly blocked out the sun. She looked frantically about the deeply shadowed wharf. She was a tiny woman by English standards, and to Rani Rangaswamy, all the English people milling about the wharf appeared as giants, obscuring her view.

*There! A little hand waving!*

"Krishan!" she screamed, running toward the hand.

A plump woman in a mob cap carried Krishan away. She moved fast for a large woman. Rani darted after them, weaving in and out of the crowds of ship crews, passengers, merchants, and laborers, trying desperately to keep Krishan in sight.

A man in rough sailor clothes jostled her on her left side, almost knocking her over, then came another jostle by a well-dressed gentleman from her right, and Rani stumbled and fell on the wharf. Her hands stung, scraped and bloodied against rough wood. Her knees ached, her green saree suffered black stains where she fell, from the tar and dirt left behind by hundreds of shoes and boots and carts that crossed and crisscrossed the dock. She scrambled to her feet but couldn't see the woman or her charge, her dear Krishan.

"Krishan!" she screamed. she looked frantically about. She ran forward a few steps. She did not know which way the woman went, where the woman might have taken him. The reality of being in a strange place among strange people who spoke a language she only partially understood threatened to crush her. Her breathing grew stuttered and rapid, tears streaked her cheeks. Six months on a ship, six months of seasickness, six months of loneliness, six months of keeping a young child entertained and safe, only to lose the child on reaching his father's country!

"Krishan!" she called again, this time her voice broken, hopeless. Fear clutched at her insides. How could she have lost him? Bringing him to England was to protect him!

She looked about her, turning in a slow circle. The air smelled of coal tar, wet wood, mud, and dead fish. No sunlight pierced the endless overcast sky. Everything appeared gray, brown, and black—quite unlike her home in Bombay. Krishan's orange shirt would stand out in this sea of sameness. It was not to be seen. What was she to do? Fear and hopelessness weighed in her chest. She could scarcely breathe. She could not believe this had happened, that Krishan was gone. She must find him!

A scruffy older English child stood by their luggage, looking as if he would make off with a piece.

She couldn't lose their luggage as well. It was all they had.

"No!" she yelled, running back to their things. The urchin who had been eyeing the alone luggage looked up. He turned to run.

"No, wait, please!" Rani yelled.

Uncertain, the boy stopped, but stood tense, ready to run, looking from her to the luggage and back.

"Help me, help me, please! I pay you. I have money!" she said, desperate for attention and help. She prayed he understood her accented English.

The child turned and ran off.

Rani collapsed against their luggage. "Krishan," she cried. Huge, shuddering sobs wracked her slight frame. *What should I do?* The horror stymied her. She couldn't think around the fact Krishan was gone.

She reached out to those who passed by, seeking help, seeking a connection with another person.

People glanced furtively her way and moved on. She dropped her head in her hands and wept.

"EXCUSE ME, Miss. Can I help you? Do you speak English?"

Rani raised her head and turned to look over her left shoulder to see the man who'd spoken. His voice had been soft but infused with concern.

"Yes, I speak English," she said, "but slowly."

The man held out his hand to her. "Here, let me help you up."

She looked at his hand, uncertain, then hesitantly

placed hers in his, and with one hand on their largest trunk, pushed herself up. She looked at the man carefully. He looked much like the clerks who worked for the East India Company in Bombay. He was tall, but not perhaps as tall as she had supposed while sitting on the ground. His hair was a light brown, his eyes gray like the clouds above, though they glinted with specks of green. He wore a neat brown jacket and pantaloons, paired with a buff waistcoat.

"Can you help me?" she asked, clasping her hands together in front of her chest, daring to hope here was someone to trust. Inwardly, she wondered what choice did she have?

"I can try. What is the problem? Why are you crying over your luggage?"

"She took Krishan!"

"She?" the man asked.

"Yes, yes, a woman."

"Do you know her?"

"No, no! She grabbed him up." She pantomimed picking up a child. "And she run off with him. I chased them, but I fell and lost them."

"Your son?"

"No, I am his ayah, his nursemaid, you understand?" Her expression twisted with anxiety.

The man nodded. "I understand. Where are his parents?"

"His mother, she is dead, and his father, he is dying. Or he might be dead now! I don't know." Her voice rose, shrill with panic. She swallowed, nodded to herself, and in a forced, calmer tone continued. "He have me bring Krishan here, to his brother. We must find Krishan! He will be so frightened!"

"We will," the man assured her. "First, we must get you and your things off this wharf and then notify the Thames River Police and the local magistrates."

"Thames River Police? What is this Thames River Police?" Rani asked, her face screwed up in confusion at the unknown words.

"They work to prevent crime along the wharves and the river. I will get someone to take care of your luggage to keep it safe. Wait here," he said.

"Wait!" She grabbed his forearm. "Your name, please, sir?"

"Yes! Where are my manners? I am David Thornbridge of Waddley Spice and Tea Company. That is our warehouse over there." He pointed to one of the large brick buildings. "And you?"

"I am Rani Rangaswamy."

He nodded. "I'll have your things taken to the Waddley warehouse for safekeeping while we hunt for the boy. What is his name?"

"Christopher Sedgewick. His mother called him Krishan. His father, he calls him Kit."

The gentleman's eyes widened at hearing the name. "We will find him. I promise you. We will find him."

Rani looked at the English gentleman and her heart felt lighter. A tiny flame of hope flickered to life.

~

*SEDGEWICK!*

That was the Earl of Soothcoor's family name! If the child was a Sedgewick, the Earl would want heaven and earth moved to find him, no matter how remote the connection. Damn, Soothcoor would do that for any child, regardless of relationship, as would his own employer, Lady Branstoke.

David didn't know whether he should bless or curse the mudlark who'd told him about the foreigner crying. He'd had his eye on the lad for a while, wondering if he could entice him out of his thieving occupation with other work. This might be the opportunity to do so.

He spotted one of his burly warehousemen pulling an empty hogshead cart and waved him over, instructing him to have the woman's small mound of baggage stored in their warehouse.

"See that they take it to the third floor and put it to the side. Tell the clerk up there to mark it for the Earl of Soothcoor."

"Aye, sar," the man said. He immediately began loading his cart with the baggage.

David turned back to the woman beside him. "Come, we'll ask after the child and put out word for his recovery," he told her, leading her down the dock.

"How old is the boy?" he asked as they hurried forward. He had to change his pace for her. She likely didn't have her land legs yet if she'd just disembarked from the ship from India, and her petite stature would have her doing two paces to his one.

"Five," she said. "He has five summers."

"Can you give me his description?"

"Yes, yes! He is thin—the sea voyage not good for him. His hair and eyes are brown."

"What is he wearing?"

"Orange shirt. That is how I saw him. An orange shirt and light pants, like sails. And sandals. Oh, his feet will get so cold here," she lamented.

David looked down at her green and gold saree and sandaled feet. "So will yours. Do you have warmer clothes?"

"No, no. Sahib, he give me money and say I must buy clothes in England."

"What did he tell you to do when you got here? Did no one know you were coming?"

She shook her head. "No, there was no time," she said. "He believe he was dying. He say to go to his brother. He give me the address and a letter for him. I sent it when the ship dock, but no one comes," she said, her brow furrowing with her sad frown.

David silently swore. If ever there was a more fraught situation, he didn't know what it was. Two weeks ago, *The Times* reported the Earl of Soothcoor numbered among the London residents who had left the city until the new year. Would any of his London staff be at his residence, or would they have left the city as well? Many London residents left a minimum staff in their London townhomes when they were away. They took the rest of the staff with them or gave them holidays, depending on the time of year and how long the family intended to be away from the city.

"I am afraid it is likely he is not in town," he gently told her.

She looked at him, stricken. "What am I to do?"

"My employer is a good friend of the Earl. I know she and her husband will help you. We will get a search on for the boy, and then I will take you to their home."

Rani's steps slowed. She bit her lower lip. What was she to do?

David looked back at her, then stopped when he noted her hesitation. "You are frightened, I know. And you don't know me; however, I vow to you I will protect you. The docks are not a safe place for you to stay."

He couldn't imagine what thoughts and emotions must harry her like dogs nipping at her heels. It would be best if she could trust him. How do you convince someone you mean them no harm when they have just had harm done to them? How does one grant trust and accept trust under confusing circumstances?

He saw when her shoulders relaxed. She nodded at him and took a deep breath, as if using the breath in and out to expel some of her fears. He hoped it did.

David led her to a small wood structure built

against the last warehouse on the wharf. It was a ram-shackle building, an afterthought to the wharf plans, built of the odd bits of construction materials left from building the wharf and warehouses in the past ten years. It was the local office of the Thames River Police.

They stopped in the doorway, their eyes adjusting to the gloom inside. One man in blue uniform pants and jacket stood behind a rough wood counter, leaning his elbows on it as he read a newspaper spread out before him.

"Excuse me," David interrupted from the entrance.

The man hastily looked up and stuffed the paper behind him.

"A ship came in from India today."

"Yes, the Lady Abernathy," the man said, nodding. "Came in on the mornin' tide."

"Yes, yes! That is the ship!" Rani said excitedly.

David nodded. "This woman and her charge, a young boy of five, were among the passengers. While she was seeking directions to her destination, an older woman snatched the boy up."

"What was he wearing?"

"Wearing?"

"Yes, what was he wearing?" the man repeated as he pulled out paper and pencil from below the countertop.

"Orange shirt," she ran a hand down her arm to indicate long sleeves. "And light-colored pants," Rani said.

"Shoes?"

"No, just sandals. As I say to this man, Sahib says to me to buy clothes in city."

"Is the boy Indian?"

Her head bobbled. "Some," she temporized.

The man's head jerked up. "Some?"

"His father is English," David explained.

The man grunted and nodded in understanding. "His name?"

"Christopher Sedgewick," David said.

"But he is called Krishan or Kit," Rani added.

He jotted down the name.

"I believe the child is a relative of the Earl of Soothcoor," David gravely told him.

The man looked up and let out a low whistle through the gap between his front teeth.

"We need to find him," David replied.

"Yes, sir! I can spread the word, give you some ideas of where to look, report it to the office in Wapping, but you should hire yourself a Bow Street Runner, especially as he's related to the Earl."

He came from behind the counter. "Most likely he were taken for his clothes and be left somewhere naked, or if the woman has a spit o'decency, in rags."

"For his clothes?" David asked.

"Yes, sir. Those the most desperate steals the child fer their clothes, strips them, then sells the togs fer pennies to the pawnbrokers. Leaves the hapless tots where they stripp'd 'em, sometimes close to a pawnbroker."

Rani's brow furrowed as she tried to closely follow what the man said. She understood English better than she spoke it—especially when she was stressed—but sometimes they used words she did not know. What was this pawnbroker? She looked up at Mr. Thornbridge.

"Thank you. That's most helpful," David said. He reached into his pocket. "Here's a few of my cards, if you would be so good as to pass the word on to your associates."

"Certainly sir, and good luck to you."

David led Rani away from the makeshift office.

"What is this pawnbroker?" she asked softly.

"A shop for lending money for goods. If the goods are not retrieved in a certain amount of time, the pawnbroker sells them."

"Like a bank?" she asked.

David laughed. "Yes, a bit like a bank, I suppose, that lends money based on assets, but on a much different scale, and they are not in the best parts of the city."

"What do we do now?" she asked.

"We contact Bow Street and get the runners involved. They will be better equipped than we are to find the boy. Come."

He grimly led her away from the wharf. He was glad that she did not question where they went or what they would do next. He wasn't sure himself what was the best course of action. He had come to hate the wharves, and only agreed to continue to work for Waddley Spice and Tea until Lady Branstoke sold it. There was greed and poverty and cruelty in and around the business of shipping. It revolted him. Sometimes he had nightmares of the attack he'd suffered on the wharves, paid for by supposed gentlemen of the *ton* after he had discovered their vile business of selling and shipping young women overseas for sex. But he'd promised Lady Branstoke he would stay with the company, and he would, until she could complete the sale, so they could both be free of it. But what he would do afterward, he did not know.

He would like to leave the city and perhaps be an estate steward or a peer's secretary. When he was younger, and home from school, he used to follow the nearby Larchside estate steward around and pepper him with questions about the estate, which at the time had been in decline. But life after school took him elsewhere. Now, however, he attended every lecture he could on the latest theories on growing crops and livestock husbandry, to educate himself about his new goal.

Life certainly had twists and turns. He remembered how proud he'd been to secure a position with Waddley

Spice and Tea. Now he grew restless for his next position.

He hurried Miss Rangaswamy, as best he might, to the street. A couple of blocks away from the wharf, they secured a hackney and were on their way to Bow Street.

# CHAPTER TWO

The carriage halted with a jangle of reins and a small jolt, shaking Rani from her thoughts. She looked out the carriage window. They were on a street bounded on either side by brick and stone-block buildings. The street was full of carriages, people walking purposefully, and merchants calling out their wares and services. It differed from the dock sounds—louder. Some would call it noisy. Rani felt comforted by it, especially after the monotonous sounds of the sea voyage. She hadn't realized how much she had missed the sounds of the city's comings and goings.

David climbed out of the carriage first and then extended her a firm gloved hand. Catching her balance on the cobbles—after six months aboard a ship, it would take her a while to lose her sea legs—Rani looked wide-eyed and anxiously about at the people, horses, and coaches crowding the street.

She swiftly readjusted the pallu—the loose, embroidered end of her green saree—over her head and hurried after Mr. Thornbridge, afraid she would lose sight of him as she had Krishan. This London place was cold and gloomy in fall—a world the color of ash. The heavy stone weight she'd felt on the dock yet sat in her chest, threatening to steal her breath away. Her head ached from her tears, her cheeks papery dry. She hadn't eaten at all that day, too excited to break her fast that morning as the ship sailed up the river to port. Then there had been a bit of sun breaking through the clouds, glittering on the water swells as, on the early morning high tide, the ship navigated the Thames River passage to the dock. But the sun hid as the sailors scurried to secure the ship to the wharf. The pleasant breeze that had ruffled her saree as she stood on deck, lifting her face to the sun, had become an unpleasant, chilly wind. She pulled the layers of the light saree fabric tighter about her body.

At least she'd ensured Krishan had food that morning.

Sahib had not adequately prepared her for the voyage or their arrival in England. He had been so insistent they leave India as soon as possible so his son would not see him die. She felt ignorant, like the verist peasant. Her confidence in herself, and the confidence Mr. Sedgewick had in her, had been real six months ago when Krishan and she had left India. How naïve she had been. And still was!

The sea journey had not agreed with either of them. They both lost weight. And though she tried to ensure they walked the deck every day for exercise, many times the weather did not favor their walks. Krishan slept fitfully, countless times crying himself to sleep while clutching his mother's singing bird music box that no longer worked. He never had a good sleep, and therefore she did not as well. He didn't understand why they had left his father and his home, didn't understand why they were on the ship day after day. He had always been a sunny child, but the changes had eroded his sunny nature and made him fearful. She well understood the change; still, she hoped to one day see him happy again.

The other passengers on the ship had kept to themselves, some looking at them with raised eyebrows but not a word said to them. There were no other Indian passengers, only the lascars hired as sailors, and they were too busy to speak. Rani found herself depressed with fears and uncertainties—her old demons—returning. Why did they have to leave India? That is what she now wondered. But Sahib had been so insistent there was no time to think, just to do. She chided herself, for her fears were her weakness, yet she couldn't shake them off.

During the long sea voyage, she'd thought often about Sahib's illness. It was not like anything she had seen or heard of before. He just became sicker and sicker. By the time they left, his hair was falling out and he could scarcely rise from his bed.

She wanted to search for Krishan herself; however, she knew she would be of no help for him and would be as lost as he in this strange, new place. She would have to trust this stranger. He'd been the only one to show her kindness. The knowledge somersaulted her stomach. She would do what she must each day, and each moment at a time she would weigh her options for the best for Krishan. At least this stranger, this Mr. Thornbridge, seemed to know of the Sedgewick family and that they had some importance in this country.

David stopped and turned toward her. When she came to his side, he took her hand and tucked it in the crook of his arm, all without saying a word. She looked up at him, hoping he could see the gratitude in her expression. He nodded and led her to a large, gray, stone-block building that dominated the street. He led her up its shallow steps to heavy, dark wood double doors.

This must be the Bow Street office he had spoken of earlier.

Voices echoed inside the cavernous room. The front half of the office where they stood was all but filled with angry and frightened people, mostly men, but a few women, and of seemingly every social status. Rani drew closer to Mr. Thornbridge. The rise and fall of voices discussing and explaining their errands was a cacophony so loud it was a wonder anyone heard anyone else above the din. At one end of the wide-open room, Rani saw a wood railing partitioning off an area where men sat behind desks and people stood in small groups before them. A man stood guard at a gate in the railing to allow people into the desk area and allow out those inside. Another man with a sheaf of papers in his hand greeted people as they came in, inquiring as to their business and directing them where to wait, or if they should leave.

"State your business," said the man with the papers, as she and Mr. Thornbridge finally inched their way forward to the front of the crowd. He scowled at them over his spectacles.

Mr. Thornbridge startled Rani when he pulled her in front of him. She looked wide-eyed up at the scowling gentleman.

"Miss Rangaswamy arrived in London this morning with her young charge, but someone has kidnapped the boy off the East India Docks," David explained.

The man gave an impatient frown. "Did you report it to the Thames River Police?"

"Yes, and they suggested we bring it to your attention."

"Damn lazy clodpoles. Now everyone wants us to do their work for them. It's their jurisdiction, not ours. We can't help you." He moved away.

Rani made an anguished sound.

"The boy is a relative of the Earl of Soothcoor," David said sharply.

"Yes, yes," Rani said, looking from the man to David and back. Her heart caught in her throat.

The man paused and looked back over his shoulder. "Soothcoor, you say. How close a relative?"

Rani stepped forward, desperate. "Lord Soothcoor be Sahib's brother," she said, wringing her hands together.

The man frowned and looked at Thornbridge. He shook his head. "What is she meaning?"

"The Sahib she mentions is her employer, Owen Sedgewick," Thornbridge explained. "He is the Earl's brother. Soothcoor is the child's uncle. Sedgewick charged Miss Rangaswamy with bringing him from India to England, so he might live with his uncle."

Rani nodded vigorously.

The man's eyebrows pulled together in a deep frown as he stood straighter and drew his head back. "Ah, that changes things. Best you talk to the Chief Clerk, Mr. Safford. He sits at the high desk. Come, I'll make sure you're next in."

He led them to the man at the railing gate, whispered something in that man's ear. The man nodded and motioned them to stand to his right. The gentleman they'd been speaking with went on through the gate and approached the high desk, deferentially standing to the side as Mr. Safford talked to two men standing before him. Safford glanced his way, nodded once, then continued with his conversation.

David made sure that his charge was out of the way of the shoving crowd, then turned his attention back to the Chief Clerk. From his gestures, it appeared Safford was dismissing the two men.

"It won't be long now," David assured Rani. He

couldn't imagine what must go through her mind. She was frightened, he could tell by her expression and posture, but she was holding herself together well, no more wailing as she'd first done. And she was cold, but did not make any complaint, her focus on the boy. He wondered what it must be like for her, a stranger in a foreign country with no support. His countrymen tended to be wary of foreigners, so it did not surprise him that people ignored her on the wharf. But he was the son of a vicar. As a young child, his father had taught him to help others in distress. He could no more ignore her than he could forget his name.

He would miss the lecture tonight at the Royal Academy of Science on the advantages of diverse crops and crop rotation. He had been looking forward to it. He was striving to learn as much as he could about land and estate management. He had to, if he wanted to leave London and the dockyards behind.

A moment later, the gatekeeper motioned them through as the two men who'd been pleading their case to the Chief Clerk exited. They didn't look satisfied with the results of their meeting with Mr. Safford. David hoped their errand would have a better outcome. Without help from Bow Street, David did not know how they would find the child.

"Mr. Spenser tells me you have lost something of the Earl of Soothcoor's," Mr. Safford said severely without preamble once they stood before his high desk.

"Yes, sir," David began.

"Yes, yes," Rani echoed beside him. And then, before he had a chance to stop her, she gripped the front edge of the desk to pull herself up to stand as tall as she might.

"Miss Rangaswamy!" David exclaimed softly, as he discreetly tried to pull her back.

Mr. Safford's mouth curved into a reluctant, crooked smile. "It is all right, sir. I understand her desire to see whom she is speaking to. My desk is high." He looked up. "Mr. Spenser, if you please," he called out. "Something for the lady to stand on."

A startled Mr. Spenser rushed to bring a chair up to Mr. Safford's desk. When the heavy wood chair was placed in front of the desk, Rani looked at it askance, seemingly not sure how to climb onto it as the seat was higher than her knees.

Seeing her challenge, David stepped closer. He held his hands out. "If you will excuse my boldness, Miss Rangaswamy, I shall lift you up to stand on the chair," he offered.

Rani's face blossomed into a smile, its brilliance catching him like a hard thump to his chest. He couldn't help but smile. He hoped not inanely.

"Yes, yes. Please," she said.

David put his hands on her waist and picked her up. She was light, and through the voluminous folds of fabric wrapped about her, he could tell she was thin. Too thin. Why so many layers of fabric? It couldn't be for warmth, as the bulk of the fabric was just wrapped and folded around her middle.

"Thank you," she said simply, with none of the embarrassment David knew an English woman would have displayed should she need to be picked up. And then, somewhat to his surprise, she took charge of the situation.

"I am Krishan's ayah, his nursemaid, you understand?" she said to Mr. Safford. She twisted her fingers together. "I bring him to England. Sahib, his father, he says *bring Krishan to my brother*," she said, those last words mimicking her employer's lower tone. "Except he called him Kit, not Krishan like me and his mother."

"And what is the lad's actual name?"

"Sedgewick, sir. Christopher Sedgewick. He is five years."

Safford nodded and took notes. David chafed at the slow process of the interview but held his tongue. He'd been surprised but pleased that the Chief Clerk had allowed Miss Rangaswamy to take the lead. Most men in his position would have deferred to the male—particularly the English male—and ignored the Indian woman.

"And what is young Christopher's father's name?" Safford asked.

"Sahib? He is Mr. Sedgewick."

"His given name."

"Given name?" Her eyes widened. "I do not know!" she said. She shook her head and frowned as she looked down. "How is it I do not know?" she said with heavy consternation.

"Owen," David Thornbridge supplied. "Owen Sedgewick is heir to the Earl of Soothcoor. I believe there are other younger brothers. I know nothing about them."

Safford nodded and took more notes.

"So how is it you are in England now, Miss—" he glanced down at his notes, "Rangaswamy?" he asked.

"Sahib, he very sick. Doctor say he will not live. Sahib say to take Krishan to England to his brother. Everything happen so fast! He give me money and papers, and next day we are on ship. No time to think, just go."

"And what happened today?"

"I sent Sahib's letter to his brother when the ship docked. The lascars—my countrymen who work on ship—they put our boxes and trunks on the dock and left us. I am afraid. Hours pass. No one from Sahib's brother's house come to help. Krishan, I tell him to sit on trunk while I ask someone on dock how to get to our new home. While I try to find a person who will talk to me, Krishan call my name."

She paused and swallowed hard. "A woman, she picks him up and runs down the dock with him. I try to follow, but I fall and lose them. I am crying, crying. I don't know what to do. This man, Mr. Thornbridge, he come to help, and I am here."

"I took her to the Thames River Police," David interjected, taking up the tale. "They took notes and said they would be on the lookout, but they suggested we come to Bow Street for help. The River Police suggested the woman took him for his clothes."

Mr. Safford nodded. "Yes, a common crime in London these days. The culprit could leave him anywhere in the city," he said grimly. Then his eyes narrowed. He looked out across the room. "Spenser! Get me Mr. Martin."

The same man who had brought the chair immediately left off speaking to the people standing before him and went through a door at the back of the room.

Safford nodded in satisfaction. "Lewis Martin knows the best and the worst of London and can easily move between both worlds. He is in high demand as an investigator."

David knew that meant Mr. Martin expected to be well paid for his investigation. "I understand," he said.

Safford grunted in response.

A moment later, a blond tousle-haired gentleman approached the desk. David thought he was about his own age, maybe a little older than himself. He dressed much like any City of London bank clerk. David could see him talking with the higher end of society, but the lower end? David had his doubts.

"You sent for me, sir?"

"Yes, Martin. These people need your help. The Earl of Soothcoor's nephew has been kidnapped off the East

India Docks today." He looked over at Rani. "How old did you say he was?"

"Five, he is five."

"Yes." He looked back at Mr. Martin. "Find him."

Lewis raised an eyebrow at him, then cocked his head. "Yes, sir."

# CHAPTER THREE

"This way."

Lewis guided them through the same door they'd seen Mr. Spencer go through. He picked up a lantern from a listing wooden side table, then led them down a darkened hall to a bare, dusty room scarcely larger than a larder. The chamber was empty save for a battered wooden desk that took up half the space and a single chair built for utility and not comfort. He placed the lantern on the bare desk and motioned for Miss Rangaswamy to sit.

Rani tentatively sat down, her large, brown eyes with their anxious expression lit by the pool of lantern light.

Lewis leaned against the wall. "Now tell me everything," he said, his voice low but intense. "Leave nothing out," he instructed. "Tell me what you saw, what you did, what you heard. Everything."

For the fourth time that day, she repeated her story and the Bow Street Runner listened intently, his arms crossed and two fingers of his right hand resting lightly on his lips as she spoke, his blue eyes never leaving her face.

"Describe him," he said.

"He is so high," she said, holding her hand a few inches above the desktop. "Thin. He lost much weight on the ship. Brown eyes, dark hair like mine." She wrinkled her nose, "And too long, he not let me cut it much."

"And what of his skin tone?"

"He is like me," she said, pointing to the skin color of the back of her hand. "Some call us *kutcha-butcha*. Not nice," she said sadly.

"Kutcha-butcha? What is that?" he asked.

"He is not Indian and not English. Like half-baked child, that is what *kutcha-butcha* mean. That is what they call us," she said with a deep sigh.

"Yes, as you say, not nice at all. You have an English father as well?"

She nodded. "I did."

Lewis Martin caught her change in tense. He frowned.

Her lips compressed into a tight line. She looked down. "It is hard to be *kutcha-butcha*," she said softly, "neither belonging to one or the other." She looked up. "Sahib, he didn't care I was *kutcha-butcha*. He hired me to care for Krishan."

He nodded. "I understand." He looked over at David Thornbridge. "And, sir, how did you become involved?"

"A mudlark alerted me there was a woman who needed help," David explained.

"Does this mudlark have a name?"

"Dan Wright, at least that is what I've been able to wrest from him."

Lewis gave a short laugh as he straightened and pushed away from the wall. "Daniel Wrightson. About ten to twelve years of age, hair more red than brown, favors a plaid cap."

David smiled and nodded. "That's the boy."

David watched the runner take a deep breath, then let it out slowly. He ran a hand through his tousled hair.

"Good. That might be the best break we have," Lewis said.

"Why do you say that?" David asked.

"Lad's observant."

"That has been my thought in my dealings with him down on the wharf. He's impressed me. I think he's smart, too smart for a guttersnipe."

"That he is," Lewis agreed. "You don't know the half of it."

David saw a corner of the man's lips kick up. He appeared to savor unshared knowledge of the lad. David felt a twinge of pique at the man's greater familiarity.

"I'd like to see him do something other than scrounging the mudflats at low tide and catching whatever the ship's crew throws overboard," he said.

"Agree," the runner said. "But now, we'd best be to it. I need to contact my informants to get them searching —including young Wrightson. Where can I find you?"

David pulled a card from his pocket and handed it to Lewis. "This has the location of my rooms, and the second address is my office."

"Waddley Spice and Tea," Lewis read on the card. His eyes narrowed as he studied David.

David sighed. "Yes, I was involved in that mess earlier in the year. My employer, the former Mrs. Waddley, now Lady Branstoke, asked me to investigate her late husband's death."

"I've read the reports," Lewis said. "Nasty business, that. And what of Miss Rangaswamy? Where might I find her if necessary?"

"I know the Earl is not currently in residence in London; consequently, I plan to take her to Sir James Branstoke's townhouse. It's just off Berkley Square. I know that is what Lady Branstoke would want. Though they are not currently in town, at least they are closer."

David gave a short, wry laugh. "If I didn't take Miss Rangaswamy to them, I'm sure I would receive a chilling dressing down from my lady. But I expect the Branstokes will be in London before nightfall tomorrow."

Lewis nodded. He looked over at Miss Rangaswamy. "We will find him," he assured her, his tone soft and—David thought—surprisingly kind.

~

OUTSIDE THE BOW STREET OFFICE, the temperature had plunged with approaching night. Rani tried to conceal her shivering from Mr. Thornbridge. As a servant, it would not do to draw attention to herself. In India, she had learned that the hard way with her previous employer and the bruises she received. She grabbed the edges of the fabric of her pallu over her head and held it together under her chin.

*I am no one*, she reminded herself. She hadn't been brought up to know that; however, she quickly learned her place when her cousin turned her out of her uncle's house and she'd had to seek employment.

*I am no one!*

It was Krishan who must command her thoughts.

She let Mr. Thornbridge hand her up into a hackney carriage and took the rear-facing seat. She bowed her head down, huddling into herself, determined to ignore the cold like her uncle Abhijit and the other ascetics of her country could do. But her body convulsively shivered, and tears leaked from the corners of her eyes at her weakness.

"My God! You are freezing!" David exclaimed, his

voice rough. He unbuttoned his coat and shrugged out of it. "Come here, let me wrap this around you," he said as he pulled her over to his seat and draped the coat around her shoulders.

"No! No!" she protested, pushing the coat away.

"Yes! What good should you be to your charge if you should catch a chill?" he asked. "How stupid can I be that I have not seen how cold you must be, and you have borne it without a word," he remonstrated himself aloud. He wrapped his coat around her shoulders, pulling the edges together in front of her, buttoning two buttons to cocoon her within its folds, and pushing the collar up alongside her head. When he was happy at her wrapped appearance, he leaned back in his seat.

Rani wanted to reject the coat. She wanted to be as the other ascetics, denying her body's discomfort, but the warmth of his body still radiated within the fabric of the coat. She savored the warmth but berated herself. How wicked was it for her to enjoy the little comfort with Krishan missing?

She looked down at her lap. She hoped Krishan had found some warmth. She was terrified for him. But what could she do? Was she wrong to trust this stranger? She did not know what to do or not do. Sometimes her fear rose in her throat, threatening to strangle her. But then she prayed, and the vision of Krishan's sweet face came to her mind to calm her. She closed her eyes as more silent tears ran down her checks.

~

DAVID LOOKED out the carriage window. They were near the Branstoke townhouse. With the Branstokes at Summerworth Park, the knocker might be off the door.

If it was down, they would need to go to the back servants' entrance. Best to assume it was down.

He rapped on the carriage roof. The driver slowed the carriage and opened the hatch.

"Yes, guvnor?"

"Let us off at the mews entrance instead."

"Certainly, sir." The roof hatch closed.

David settled back in the seat next to Rani. "The door knocker will be down—they won't hear us at the front of the house. We'll go through the mews to the back entrance."

He looked at her huddled in his coat. "Are you all right, miss?"

She nodded briskly. "Just so much to think. My mind is full and fearful," she sorrowfully said.

"I know. Mine, too. But we need to think positively. To have faith. You have come a long distance with determination and grace. It will not be for naught. You shall see," he whispered, hoping he was right. He could not imagine what this tiny woman has endured since she left India, traveling alone with a young child coming to a strange country. And now this tragedy of the lost boy. And not just because he was Soothcoor's nephew.

David felt the carriage slow and then stop again. He reached across Rani to open the door. He rose, looking out at the empty street. The lamplighters had been down the street, though it wasn't full night yet. Small pools of light lined the street while the maw of the mews entrance remained dark. He hopped down from the carriage, then turned to help her down.

So enveloped in his coat, she looked like a tree sapling. David had to smile. With her arms enclosed, he knew she could not reach for his hand to help her descend from the carriage. He picked her up as he had at the Bow Street office and set her down on the pavement.

"Thank you," she said simply, as if that method of descending a carriage was an everyday occurrence. He paid the hackney driver, then gently laid a hand at the small of her back to guide her to the mews entrance.

Inside the mews alley, the houses and stables on either side blocked out the last remnants of twilight. In the mews it appeared night had fallen, yet few of the night lanterns had been lit. David guided Rani through the darkness, past horse stalls and broken bits of household castoffs. It smelled of refuse and horse dung, but the area was slightly warmer than on the street. No wind blew through the mews, blocked as it was by the buildings all around.

He slowed as they came halfway down the length of the mews. He studied the backs of the townhouses, uncertain in the dark which one was the back of the Branstoke townhouse.

"Can I help you, sir?" said a voice from the darkness of the stables behind them.

David turned to make out the figure in the dark.

A click and an orange light spark in the dark revealed the man's location. He was lighting a lantern to hang on a sturdy oak wood beam. Behind him, a horse neighed softly and shuffled in the straw.

David thought he recognized the man.

"Romley?" he asked. He drew Rani toward the man hanging the lantern. "George Romley, correct?"

"Ah, 'tis you, Mister Thornbridge," George Romley said affably.

David watched his eyes slide from him to the Indian woman beside him.

"But what are you doing here? Sir James and Lady Branstoke are in Kent," Romley said, looking back at David.

"I know. I'm looking for a way into the Branstoke house, but from the back, I can't tell which is their house."

George Romley chuffed. "'Tis the one on the right."

"Thank you," David said, and turned toward the specified house.

"What's the lay, sir?" Romley asked.

He looked uncomfortable with their presence in the mews, and David thought he didn't blame him. But he didn't answer him directly. "Can you take a message to the Branstokes in the morning?" he asked

Romley was silent a moment as he pulled his tobacco pouch from his vest pocket. "Yes, sir. I can leave at first light," Romley finally said, as he pulled a pinch of tobacco out.

"Good. Tell them a child was kidnapped today from the East India Docks."

Romley jerked upright, tobacco flying from the open pouch. "The docks! Bloody 'ell! They'll be in town before tomorrow night. Her ladyship will see to that!" Romley averred.

"I'm counting on it," David said grimly.

# CHAPTER FOUR

$\mathcal{D}$avid lifted the latch on the iron gate at the rear of the Branstoke townhouse property and led Rani into the back garden. The garden space wasn't big, just an overgrown kitchen garden beside a narrow, uneven brick walk that led to the steps down to the servants' and tradesmen's entrance.

David pounded on the backdoor leading to the townhouse kitchen, then took a step back. Rani stood on the step above him, her head peeping around him.

They heard a bolt slide back, and then the door opened quickly.

"Romley! What do you—" the aggravated butler began, then stopped. He squinted at them, seeing them by the light spilling out from the kitchen behind him. "Oh, sorry, sir. I thought it was George Romley banging on the door." He straightened, resuming his formal butler manner and tone. "I'm afraid the Branstokes are not in residence."

"I know, Charwood. I need somewhere for Miss Rangaswamy to stay tonight."

Charwood scowled. "Now see here!"

Rani shrank back from David and hunched in his oversized coat as if she could disappear inside it.

"Easy, Charwood." David said, extending his hand outward. "You should know me better than that!" he said sharply.

First Romley and now Charwood. They need to get their minds out of the gutter.

"Miss Rangaswamy's young charge has been kidnapped off the East India Docks, and the person she was to see once she arrived in London is out of the city. Under the circumstances, and knowing Lady Branstoke, I felt this was the safest place for her. I would appreciate your cooperation," he said in his most repressive tone, the one he typically reserved for supercilious merchants who thought to cheat the company because they knew the company was now owned by a woman.

Mrs. Dunstan, the housekeeper, peeked around Charwood's broad frame.

"Of course, Mr. Thornbridge," Mrs. Dunstan enthused on identifying him. The middle-aged housekeeper, though of slight frame, shouldered past the broad-shouldered butler to beckon them inside. "Do come in, both of you. It is too cold outside at this time of night to be dickering on the steps."

Charwood harrumphed and reluctantly moved aside for them to enter.

David found Mrs. Dunstan's reception surprising, but welcoming. She and Charwood were often at odds for their dignities and position in the household. Typically, she was the skeptical, foreboding person. It was gratifying to see the reverse, as Miss Rangaswamy needed kindness.

They stepped into the kitchen. With the thick exterior door closed behind them, they immediately felt the room's warmth and smelled food cooking on the cast iron stove set into a gigantic fireplace. David saw Rani momentarily close her eyes and a small smile touch the corners of her lips. A deep breath expelled on a sigh between her lips. She shrugged out of David's coat and handed it back to him.

"Thank you, sir," she said in a whisper. She gracefully removed the pallu from over her head and draped it around her shoulders.

Charwood looked her up and down, sneered, and looked away.

"Oh, my gracious! Is that all you have for clothing?" Mrs. Dunstan exclaimed at seeing Rani's exotic saree. "You must be frozen, despite Mr. Thornbridge's coat. Do you have anything else to wear, you poor thing?"

Rani sighed and shook her head. "No, ma'am," she said. "I have money from Sahib to buy English clothes. Everything I have is like what I wear now. Mr. Thornbridge, he have our luggage put away to keep safe."

Mrs. Dunstan looked at David.

"This Sahib she speaks of is her employer in India, Owen Sedgewick, the Earl of Soothcoor's brother."

"Soothcoor?" Charwood said, his head coming up to stare at Rani.

"Yes, Miss Rangaswamy brought Soothcoor's nephew to England to live with Soothcoor. The child was stolen off the dock this morning," David grimly told them.

Mrs. Dunstan raised a hand to her lips as her eyes widened and she bit back an exclamation.

Charwood swore viciously.

"Of course, you must stay here!" Mrs. Dunstan said, "And you must be starving!" She turned toward the large fireplace with its built-in ovens and cast-iron stove. "I have a stew on the stove now. Let me just add a few more vegetables, and while they are cooking, we shall find something of madam's you can wear."

"What? Never!" Charwood exclaimed.

"What is it now, Mr. Charwood?" Mrs. Dunstan demanded, arms akimbo, as she faced him down. "I don't understand what has gotten into you. What is your issue?"

"You would give this—this *foreigner* her ladyship's clothes?"

Mrs. Dunstan tilted her head quizzically. "And why not? Why is it even a question? I'll own I have not always agreed with those Sir James and Lady Branstoke have brought to the house; however, I have learned to trust our employers—and Mr. Thornbridge. And so should you."

"Yes, but this woman—"

Rani stepped back, closer to David.

David touched her arms to reassure her. He felt Mrs. Dunstan had the upper hand and felt no reason to abut the discussion. He rather enjoyed it.

"There is no *But*, Mr. Charwood," Mrs. Dunstan ringingly declared. "You forget yourself. For one," she held up one finger, "the Earl of Soothcoor is a good friend to Sir James and my lady. And second," a second finger went up, "Lady Branstoke does not hold with herself or anyone else being better than another," she said sharply, shaking a finger at him. "Now, dinner," she said, as she pulled out a couple of potatoes and carrots from the larder. She fetched a knife from a sideboard.

"Here, peel these and add them to the pot while I tend to Miss Rangaswamy." She thrust the knife and vegetables into Charwood's hands.

"No! How dare you suggest that!" Charwood protested, fumbling to hold the vegetables and knife at the same time.

David laughed. "I'll help you, Charwood. My father made me peel vegetables many a time as a punishment for one youthful misdeed or another. I believe I still know how to do that. I admit I am famished, and I should like to see Miss Rangaswamy settled." He crossed to the sideboard and retrieved another knife.

"On your way, Mrs. Dunstan. We have things in hand here," David said, waving her off with the tip of the knife.

He looked at Rani. "Go with Mrs. Dunstan, Miss Rangaswamy," he gently said. "As I told you earlier, you will do Krishan no good if you should take a chill. Warmer clothes and a hot meal are what you need right now."

Mrs. Dunstan put her arm around Rani as she escorted her out of the room.

David peeled a potato. "Charwood!" he said, drawing the man to the task at hand. "What is the matter?" he asked.

Charwood lifted his head up and sniffed. "I am the butler, not the kitchen maid," he said austerely.

"Well, I don't see any maids about," David said. "Have they all gone down to Summerworth Park or given time off?"

"No. The Branstokes sent two to visit their families while they are in Kent, and the third has her night off." He frowned. "Probably out with one of the footmen. I should put a stop to that!"

David paused in his peeling and turned his head to look fully at Charwood. "Why?" he asked simply.

Charwood harrumphed. "We'll not have any by-blows in this household!" he declared.

"I'd wager a monkey that is not what really is eating at you this evening. It is about Miss Rangaswamy, isn't it?" he said, as he dropped one potato in the stew pot and picked up another to peel.

Charwood peeled a carrot, his motions sharp and staccato, cutting away more carrot than skin.

David knew he was trying to ignore the question.

He grabbed the man's forearm. Charwood looked over at him, frowning.

David took the carrot from him. "You are not peeling that carrot—you are mutilating it. What is your issue with Miss Rangaswamy?"

"She's from India!"

"Yes," David mildly agreed. "And?"

Charwood pulled his arm free and picked up another vegetable. "Nothing. I just don't like foreigners."

David could tell there was something more to it than just a dislike of foreigners. Obviously, something in Charwood's past shaded his behavior. Odd, for he'd always taken Charwood to be a superior butler and a canny individual. He knew Sir James trusted the man.

"Well, you need to amend your ways to this woman," he told him. "She has done nothing to you, and she is in the Earl of Soothcoor's employ now. And you know Lady Branstoke will take her in."

Charwood took in a deep breath, then chuffed it out harshly. "Yes, sir," he said gratingly. Then he paused, and in a quieter tone he grumbled, "Yes, she will indeed."

~

"How long did the voyage take to get from India to England?" Mrs. Dunstan asked, as she led Rani to the broad carpeted stairway and up to the second floor.

"Six months. And it was quiet."

"Quiet? But there were other people on the ship."

Rani nodded in faint agreement. "But when the men do not call out to each other, or passengers not talking or walking on deck, the only sound is lapping of water on hull, and wood creaking. And it is always there, even when people about. Always the same."

Mrs. Dunstan canted her head as she considered the

sounds. "I suppose that could be eerie if one were alone, as you were."

"I did have Krishan," Rani said.

"I know, dear, but sometimes a body needs more than a child for company.... Here's madam's room," she said, as they came to the top of the third flight of stairs.

Mrs. Dunstan led Rani into Lady Branstoke's dressing room.

Rani paused in the doorway. "This is the Lady's room?"

"Yes, this is madam's dressing room. Come in. We will find you something to wear, and then I will show you to the nursery suite."

"It is very beautiful," Rani said, looking around and taking in the elegant shades of the blue décor of the dressing room. "And it smells nice. Not heavy smell."

Mrs. Dunstan smiled. "It is actually quite plain compared to some households I've been in. Lady Branstoke is not a frivolous woman. What you smell is lavender. She says it is soothing for her."

Rani nodded, "It is. I want to just stand, close my eyes, and smell."

Mrs. Dunstan smiled, delighted at Rani's reaction to Lady Branstoke's dressing room. She crossed to a large, white-painted armoire, trimmed with gold gilt, that stood in the corner.

"Would you prefer a black or gray dress? I'm afraid that is all that is here," she said, looking through a small stack of folded gowns stored in a lower drawer. "These were her mourning clothes. Madam has no need of these now." She pulled out two dresses, shook them out, and laid them across the back of a light blue damask covered settee. She looked from the dresses to Rani, then back. She picked up the gray dress.

"This one will be better for you," she said. "Go behind the screen to try it on while I look for a chemise and a night rail."

Rani took the dress from her. "It is heavy!" she said in surprise.

"Compared to the fabric of your Indian dress, I imagine it is," Mrs. Dunstan agreed. "But it will keep you warmer," said the practical woman. "Here is a chemise to go with it. Let me know when you get it on, and I will help you with the laces. Unlike Mr. Charwood and his obsession with his dignity, I am not averse to being a helping maid when the need arises," she said, with a nod and pursed lips.

Rani nodded and slipped behind the screen. She unwrapped her saree, careful to remove the papers and money she had secured within the fabric folds. She hadn't read the documents Sahib gave her. She was proud she could read English, thanks to her uncle allowing her to assist in his schoolroom. Still, she would not read documents Sahib gave her without permission.

She put the dress on, surprised to see it was not too long and only a little loose on her. She gathered up the lengths of her green saree and draped it over the screen before she came out to have Mrs. Dunstan assist her with the dress fastenings.

"Yes, this will do," Mrs. Dunstan said. "When we get you your own clothes, we will ensure they have front fastenings."

Rani felt self-conscious under Mrs. Dunstan's critical eye. She understood servants did not have dressers and felt uncomfortable with the need for the dress she wore.

"Turn around so I can lace the back."

Mutely, Rani did as she requested, feeling like the child with a nursemaid, instead of being a nursemaid.

"Is that one long length of fabric?" Mrs. Dunstan

asked, nodding toward Rani's saree as she pulled on the dress laces.

Rani's head bobbled. "Yes, yes," she said. "That one was Memsahib's, my mistress's. Sahib say I need to look good on the journey, so I am not, hmm—abused, he say. I'm to take Memsahib's clothes, as they are better than mine."

"This Memsahib, she is deceased?" Mrs. Dunstan asked.

"Yes, over a year," Rani said sadly. "She nice to me, both she and Sahib nice to me."

"How do you keep it on? Aren't you afraid it would, well, fall off?" the woman asked.

Rani laughed a little, releasing the sadness she'd felt thinking of her employers. "I have a blouse and petticoat under my saree, as that is as the British in India say is proper. We use tucking, pleating, and pins to arrange and hold our sarees and to drape our pallu," she explained, mimicking with her hands the motions of tucking, pleating, and pinning her saree.

"Pallu?"

"The cloth on the shoulder. It can cover the head and be a shawl as I wore or used to carry children."

"I hadn't realized that was all the same length of fabric. That is quite long."

Rani looked over at her saree. She frowned. The wider and longer-length saree allowed her to create the secure folds for the money and papers she carried. She shook her head. "I don't like saree that long. But it was necessary." How will she carry money and papers without saree? Reticules she see English women carry look too small.

Mrs. Dunstan finished tying the dress and stepped back. "I don't believe madam's shoes will fit. Your feet are larger than hers.

"It's all right. I wear sandals."

"Well, let's gather your things and take them to the nursemaid's room. I had it cleaned and decorated once Sir James married—just in case, you know," she confided.

Rani giggled at that.

"Then we had best get back to the kitchen. Hopefully, the gentlemen will have succeeded in their task."

Rani laughed louder. "That Mr. Charwood, he not be happy."

"No, I don't understand it; it is not like him, but don't you let it fret you. It's alright," Mrs. Dunstan claimed. "He's been moody for over six months now. It has nothing to do with you.

~

"HERE WE ARE!" called out Mrs. Dunstan as the women returned to the kitchen. "And how have you gentlemen been getting on? Vegetables peeled and in the pot? Poor Miss Rangaswamy is famished."

David rose to his feet from the oak worktable where he and Mr. Charwood sat, sharing a pint of ale.

"In the pot and boiling," he said. He turned to Charwood and winked, then turned back to the women. "Did you doubt us? And Mr. Charwood has seen fit to pour me a mug of your delicious ale from Summerworth Park." He raised his mug before him, smiling.

He dropped his smile as he looked at Rani. "And how are you, Miss Rangaswamy? Feeling better?"

"Oh yes, sir, yes, yes," she said. "Mrs. Dunstan give me this fine dress to wear," she said, running her hands down the sides, "And shown me to a pretty little yellow-and-white room to sleep in. She says it is a nursemaid's room. But it is so fine! It has a chair that rocks," she said, rocking back and forth. "The house is so pretty," she said earnestly. "Are all houses like this?"

David and Mrs. Dunstan laughed. Charwood sneered.

"No," David said. "And the Earl's home is bigger and grander."

"Oh-h-h," she said, wide-eyed.

David looked over at Mrs. Dunstan. "I've taken the liberty of putting some water on to boil. I think Miss Rangaswamy could use a nice hot cup of tea."

"Excellent, idea, Mr. Thornbridge. I would say your father did you right in your rearing."

David smiled. "Thank you, I think."

Mrs. Dunstan bustled about the kitchen, setting out the tea things and broad, shallow bowls for their stew on the table. She pulled a white, bleached towel off a loaf of bread on the sideboard and cut them each a thick slab. "We will eat in here instead of the Servants' Hall. With so few of us in the house, we don't light the fire in there."

"That is fine with me," David said.

"Sit, child," she said, looking over her shoulder at Rani as she gathered up the slices.

David pulled out a chair for her at the table. She looked from it to him, then sat down on the edge of the chair, her hands primly positioned in her lap. She looked from one to the other, wide-eyed.

Mrs. Dunstan slid into her chair, then offered a prayer before the meal. David noted Rani bow her head for the prayer. The kitchen was quiet as they ate, the only sounds the clanking of spoons against bowls and the slurping of stew. David covertly watched Rani. She ate avidly; however, she pushed the meat to the side of the bowl. Mrs. Dunstan also noted she didn't eat the meat.

"You don't eat meat?" she asked.

Rani screwed up her nose. "Not much. I did not

have it as a child and have not liked it now," she said simply.

"Isn't that a religious taboo in India?" David asked.

"For many, yes. I was raised in my uncle's house. When he became Christian, we did, too. We could eat meat, but the price, it is high. So, we did not."

She took another spoonful of stew, then looked up at Mr. Thornbridge, then over to Mrs. Dunstan. "You are certain Sir James and Lady Branstoke will help me find Krishan?"

"Lord, child, to whisper the word 'kidnap' is to send Lady Branstoke into action. She is a tiger, that one is," Mrs. Dunstan said.

"And perforce, this sends Sir James into action to see her safe," David said drily.

Rani shook her head. "I don't understand."

"Last spring, she was convinced her former husband was murdered," said Ms. Dunstan.

"Murdered?"

"Yes. And she was determined to discover who killed him."

"She asked me to do some investigation," David said. "I discovered he was involved with a scheme to kidnap young women and sell them as concubines in the Mid-East."

"And you nearly lost your life for that discovery, too," admonished Mrs. Dunstan.

David nodded. "Sir James took it upon himself to pro-tect Lady Branstoke—who was Mrs. Waddley at the time."

"That's how they came to fall in love," Mr. Dunstan said.

"And then she was kidnapped," said David, adding drama to his words, but smiling withal.

Rani leaned forward, her eyes wide. "No! What happened?"

"Sir James rescued her, but it was a near thing. All in all, kidnapping of any innocent has her up in arms."

"I see," Rani said, thinking. She sipped some tea. She closed her eyes and relaxed in her chair. "In here," she said, tapping the side of her head, "I can hear Krishan laughing and the tumble of words when he is excited. I must hold that in my head and heart," she said, touching first her forehead and then her heart. "It makes me smile and holds my fear away a little." She looked toward the house back door. "But I know he is out there somewhere, and I am so frightened for him. I would walk every street and alley if I felt it would help me find him." Her eyes glistened.

"Mr. Martin will find him," David assured her.

"I pray for it," she whispered and gave a long sigh. The warmth of the kitchen, the comforting smells of food, relaxed her, and she felt depleted. She did not know how much longer she could keep her eyes open. "I am tired," she said abruptly.

"As I am sure you are," Mrs. Dunstan said. "Fear and stress will do that to a body. Do you remember your way to your room?"

"Yes, yes," Rani said with forced brightness, willing the exhaustion at bay. "Thank you."

She started to get up. David rose and pulled out her chair for her.

"Sleep well and try not to worry too much, though I know that will be difficult. I will return in the morning."

Rani bowed her head, then left the kitchen.

"A most remarkable woman," David said, after the door closed behind her. He looked at Charwood and Mrs. Dunstan. "She has been frightened—terrified even; however, she has stood up to her fears. You should have heard her at the Bow Street office! By her manner, you would think she would be a wallflower, but she spoke right up."

"That's foreigners, for you," growled Charwood, his chair scraping against the floor as he stood up. "Can't trust them."

"What?" David asked.

"Mr. Charwood!" remonstrated Mrs. Dunstan. "That will be enough. Madam will not accept that attitude, and well you know it."

"Bah!" the butler said. Angrily, he strode to the passageway that led to the servants' rooms. He stopped to look back at them. "You'll see, you both will." With that parting comment, he stomped down the hall.

"Well, I never!" exclaimed Mrs. Dunstan. "This is so unlike the man, and I've worked with him for three years!"

"His behavior speaks of an unknown history," David said. "Don't let it bother you, Mrs. Dunstan. Sir James and Lady Branstoke will sort it out."

"I dare say," the woman said; however, her face wore a troubled frown.

CHARWOOD QUIETLY LET himself out of the Branstoke townhouse. Mrs. Dunstan's insistence on the maids oiling the door hinges monthly served his purpose, though he thought it a nuisance task for the servants. He crossed the yard to the gate leading to the mews— another oiled nuisance—and let himself out into the mews. He climbed the outside stairs of the stable to the groomsmen's rooms. George Romley was the only one in town, the others either at Summerworth Park, the Branstokes' country home in Kent, or had been given leave to spend time with their families for the holidays.

Mr. Thornbridge had no right to ask Romley to take

messages for him. And to believe someone could kidnap a child in the daytime from a bustling dock? Bah! Worse, to claim the child was some relation to the Earl of Soothcoor. Impossible. He'd always taken Mr. Thornbridge for an intelligent man. It ground at him that he should be taken in by whatever conspiracy that Indian woman was involved in. And Mrs. Dunstan merrily taking it all in, too, and treating the woman like visiting royalty made his stomach crawl.

Blind and stupid, that's what they were. You can't trust anyone from India. His brother learned that to his demise. And they looked like the bloody thieving Romanys. At least the gypsies kept to themselves. The Indians flooded London and were getting above themselves, what with opening coffee houses and bath houses and infiltrating the service ranks, taking jobs away from the hard-working English. Damn the merchantmen for hiring the lascars in India for one-way ocean trips. It was all the fault of that East India Company. The government let them do whatever they wanted.

He pounded on Romley's door. "Wake up, Romley! Damn it, wake up you clodpoll!"

The door opened to a bleary-eyed Romley, who squinted against the light from Charwood's lantern.

"Charwood! What the bloody 'ell you want? "

Charwood pushed past Romley to come into his room. He sneered at the size and the rough wood. He turned to look at Romley. "We need to talk."

"Can't it wait until morning?"

"No, you're leaving in the morning, remember?"

"Yeah, yeah. So what is so important?"

"Did Thornbridge ask you to take a message to the Branstokes?"

"Yeah, somethin' about a kidnapping on the docks."

"Doesn't that strike you as odd, there being a kidnapping in the daytime from a busy dock? Lots of people around?"

"Didn't think much about that."

"Well, think about it. I'd wager a groat it's all a hum. A scam, probably, to extort money from the Branstokes."

Romley looked confused. "Why?"

"I don't know, but I don't believe a word of that tale. You can't trust those Indians." Charwood paced the small room.

Romley rubbed the back of his neck. "You're not makin' sense, Charwood. "

"I know what I'm saying. My brother was killed because of an Indian he thought was his friend," Charwood shouted, his eyes glistening in the lantern light. He collapsed onto Romley's bed, his head in his hands. It had been over six months since he'd learned the details of what happened to his brother, and this was the first time he ever told anyone else.

"My brother was in the Indian Army. He loved it there. Wrote to me about the landscape, the pace of life, the people, the food. He loved it all. Then his commander, Major General Ochterlony, secretly sent him and his lieutenant north on a mission. They got ambushed by the Nepalese. Ochterlony's staff officer wrote to say they tortured them, and it was three days before my brother died. It was his friend he'd written to me about, Amar from Calcutta, who betrayed them, who'd sent the message to the Nepalese."

"I'm sorry, Mr. Charwood. Does Sir James know?"

"No. I've told no one until now," Charwood said miserably.

"So why are ya here?" Romley asked.

"So you can warn the Branstokes it's all a hum!"

"How do you know it is?"

"Be reasonable, Mr. Romley, the Earl of Soothcoor's

nephew? From India? And the woman, I don't think she's any better than she should be. Too young and too pretty to be a nursemaid. And says she comes from a respectable family. I don't believe none of it, not with that gold trim on that thing she wore like a dress, and her wearing Mr. Thornbridge's coat, and so I want you to tell Sir James and Lady Branstoke."

"All right, I will. I will. Now, can I get back to sleep?"

"You believe me, don't you?"

"The only thing I believe right now is I need me sleep. But I promise I will tell them your concerns. But you should know any unusual activity on that dock will have Lady Branstoke back here quick-like, no matter your doubts." He opened the door to his room, waiting for Charwood to leave.

Reluctantly, Charwood rose from where he sat on Romley's bed. He picked up his lantern and shuffled out the door.

# CHAPTER FIVE

George Romley arrived at Summerworth Park early the next morning. He hadn't slept well after Mr. Charwood's visit, so he got up at the first lightening of the sky. He didn't know Mr. Charwood well, the man having the airs of a proper butler and better than the rest of the staff. However, he'd never struck him as a fanciful man. He clearly thought the story of a kidnapped child was a hum. And it might be. However, Romley didn't want to be the one to take that chance and fail to give proper intelligence to Sir James. Remembering his days with Sir James in the military, Branstoke always said no crumb of intelligence was too small to pass on.

Then again, he didn't think Mr. Thornbridge a fanciful gentleman, either. Very proper and serious was Mr. Thornbridge.

So he would tell Sir James and Lady Branstoke all, but he wouldn't put Mr. Charwood's intensity into his message, just as he hadn't traveled faster than normal pace.

He stabled his horse, then went in the back servant's entrance to the house. His fellow servants hailed him as they saw him enter, but he didn't stop to chat. Time enough for that later, he supposed.

He remembered to take his cap off as he went up the three steps to the living area's ground floor and walked to the breakfast room. He grinned to himself as he considered how casual he was at entering the house. He remembered the last time he'd interrupted Sir James's breakfast six months ago. Coo, but that was a ramshackle business.

With sunlight streaming over his shoulder, James sat at the table reading a newspaper as he sipped his coffee.

George Romley hesitated at the door. "Beg pardon, Sir James," the self-assurance he'd felt moments ago fleeing him. He bowed awkwardly.

James looked up. "George!" he said. He rose and gestured for him to come in. That his groomsman would come in the house to seek him out did not bode well.

"Darrell, get Mr. Romley a cup of coffee and bring the sugar bowl over, too," he instructed, remembering his man liked sugar in his coffee.

George's eyes widened. "No need, sar, I jest—"

"Sit, George."

"Yes, sar." George took the seat to the left of Sir James. Darrell placed the coffee and sugar in front of him.

"You're here sooner than I expected," James said. He nodded as Darrell silently offered to refill his coffee cup.

"I know, sar. It were a'cause of Mr. Thornbridge, sar," Romley said, intent on spooning sugar into his cup.

"Thornbridge?"

"Aye, sar." Romley nodded.

"He is not injured or ill, is he?"

George looked confused. "Mr. Thornbridge? No, sar."

"So, I take it you have seen him, and he is in good health."

"Yes, I suppose, sar."

"Excellent. Then I think whatever you have to say should wait upon Lady Branstoke."

George thought for a moment. He may have thought the Indian woman was a light-skirt at first, but not for long. And Mr. Thornbridge did work for Lady Branstoke. "Yes, sar, Lady Branstoke will want to hear."

"Darrell, please ask Lady Branstoke to join us as soon as she is available."

Darrell bowed and trotted out of the room. James could hear him clatter up the stairs. He shook his head, amused.

"Help yourself to some breakfast, as well," James directed Romley. "Cook makes food enough for a regiment."

"I thank ye, sar."

"How is everything else in London?" James asked Romley.

"Well, sar, savin' Mr. Charwood, sar." Romley shook his head. "I never seed him so bacon-brained a'fore."

"Charwood?"

"Yes, sar. Makes no sense. Everything I need to tell ya and Lady Branstoke he says is a Banbury tale, and he toll me to tell ya not to believe it!"

"Interesting," James said.

Romley nodded as he took a big bite of bacon.

"Ah, good morning, Mr. Romley. Darrell said you were here," said Cecilia as she entered the room.

George scrambled to his feet, bowing, and pulling his forelock. "Lady Branstoke."

James leaned back in his chair. "My dear, I believe that quiet you abjured is about to end," he said placidly, his eyes at half-lidded attention, a look others might take as bored. Cecilia did not. She knew this was when James was at his most canny.

She looked from James to George. "You are here early in the day. What has occurred, Mr. Romley?"

George started to wipe his mouth with the back of his sleeve, then saw Lady Branstoke slightly raise one pale brow. He remembered himself and picked up the serviette to wipe breakfast crumbs away. She smiled at him.

He took another sip of coffee. "Last night, nigh dark, when I stepped outside to blow a cloud. I saw Mr. Thornbridge come down the mews with another figure. At first I couldna tell if t'were man or woman. Then I seen it were a tiny woman, like yourself, my lady, bundled in Mr. Thornbridge's coat. An Indian woman."

"An Indian woman? Like Aisha, Lady Aldrich's maid?" Cecilia asked.

"Yes, but younger, I'm thinkin'." He waved his hand. "No matter. He asks me to bring a message to ya, which is why I'm here. He said to tell ya a child's been kidnapped from the docks."

"What?" Cecilia cried. She half rose, then sat back down again. "No. Tell me more. Tell me everything," she directed. She looked over at her husband, who nodded grimly.

"That were 'bout all I got from Mr. Thornbridge, jest that I was to hie down here this mornin' and tell ya that. But Mr. Charwood, he visited me later, and that's when it got stranger." He scratched the side of his head.

"Wait, let me get my tea," Cecilia said.

"Sit. Stay where you are. Darrell can get your tea and coffee refills for Mr. Romley and me."

Darrell immediately brought hot tea to Cecilia, along with toast. Cecilia nodded her thanks. He refilled

Sir James's and Mr. Romley's coffee and moved quietly to the side of the room by the breakfast buffet.

"Now, Mr. Romley, tell us how things got strange," James said after he watched Romley stir three more teaspoons of sugar into his coffee.

"Mr. Charwood said the Indian woman claims the child kidnapped is the Earl of Soothcoor's nephew."

"Owen's son?" James said. "I wasn't aware Owen Sedgewick had a son." He looked at Cecilia. "Owen is Soothcoor's half-brother," he explained. "Arthritis has nearly crippled him. He passionately declared he would never marry or have children for fear of passing on his arthritis pain to another."

Mr. Romley shrugged. "Mr. Charwood said he thought it all a scam, but Mr. Thornbridge was serious-like. When I first saw her with him, I may have suggested she was less than a lady. Mr. Thornbridge took me to task."

"Regardless of the young woman's morals," Cecilia said, "we have a mystery on the docks. I must return to London immediately, James. I want nothing going on that might hinder the sale of the company! And if there is a kidnapping, we must resolve it immediately regardless of who may be the subject of the kidnapping—commoner or peer."

# CHAPTER SIX

$\mathcal{R}$ ani woke to the sound of the bedroom door opening. A young maid wearing a gray dress with a white bib apron came into her room carrying a laden breakfast tray. She sat up. She felt self-conscious. She'd never had someone bring breakfast to her before, or otherwise wait on her.

"Good morning, miss," the maid said. She set the tray on a small table in the corner, then crossed to the windows to open the heavy white-and-yellow striped drapes, repurposed for the nursery from the dining room redecoration the previous summer. "Mrs. Dunstan explained how you have had a horrible time since coming to England. She said to let you sleep a bit. You were so worn to flinders, she said, and in need of a mite of pampering. That's why I brung you a tray. Mrs. Dunstan, she be a dear—so long as we do our jobs and no shirking!" She turned back to the tray. "Do you like tea or chocolate? I didn't know which you prefer, so I brought both."

"Tea, but I can—"

"No, you relax. I'll bring you your tea. Do you put anything in it?"

Rani shook her head. "No," she said softly. She felt

her cheeks grow warm. It embarrassed her for this woman to wait on her.

The maid brought her the tea, then fluffed the pillows behind her so she could lean back and relax while she drank her tea.

"Has Mr. Thornbridge returned?" she asked, eager for any word on the search for Krishan.

"No, miss, but it is early yet. My name's Dot—well, actually it is Dorothy, but everyone calls me Dot—exceptin' Lady Branstoke, she calls me Dorothy," the maid said. "Eddie is bringing up hot water for a bath for you. You should like that, I'm thinkin'."

"Yes," Rani said as she watched the maid flit about the room. "I am Rani," she said shyly.

"That's a nice name," Dot said as she kneeled down before the fireplace. "Mrs. Dunstan said you're to be Miss Rangaswamy to us. That's an exotic name," the maid prattled on, as she shoveled the ashes off the banked embers before laying on more coal to get the fire going again to warm the room. "She said as how you are from India. Coo—that's a far bit. We see such wondrous pictures in the print shops coming from India. Do you think I should like it there?" she asked artlessly, as she rose from the fireplace.

"I don't know," Rani said. She paused, then as she felt compelled to say something else to the voluble maid, she added, "it is hot."

The maid considered heat for a moment. She shook her head. "No, I don't think I should like that. Are you finished with your tea? Shall I pour you another cup?"

"No!" Rani said quickly. She threw off the bed's yellow-and-blue counterpane and swung her legs over the side of the bed. "No," she said, softer and slower. "I will eat now." She slid down off the edge of the bed.

"Right-o," said Dot.

Rani crossed to the table and sat down. "Too much!"

she exclaimed, when she saw the assortment the maid had brought.

"We didn't know what you should like, so there is a bit of everything. But no meat. Mrs. Dunstan said no meat."

Rani smiled sunnily at the girl. "Thank you," she said simply.

As she ate, Rani wondered why she was being treated as an honored guest instead of as a servant. She admitted she enjoyed it, and that brought with it a wealth of guilt. While her uncle had treated her as a member of his family and not as a servant, as a teacher, his was a modest household. He allowed her to serve in his classroom and thereby listen to what he taught his male students. Rani liked to listen.

There was a knock on the door of the adjoining room.

"That will be Eddie letting me know your bath is ready when you are, miss."

"Oh, yes, yes," Rani said, dabbing at her lips with the serviette. She rose from the table.

~

RANI HAD JUST FINISHED PUTTING her hair into a low bun at the base of her neck when there was a knock on her bedroom door.

"Yes, please," she called out, as she stood up.

Dot entered. "There is a message come for you, miss," she said, holding out a cream folded note. "Do you need me to read it for you?" she hesitantly asked.

Rani laughed lightly. "No, no. I read English."

Dot blushed. "I'm sorry, miss—"

"No, no. I am lucky. Uncle taught boys, and I listen," she said with a mischievous smile. But then a frown furrowed her brow. "I hope it is good news for Krishan." She flipped open the note. "Oh, I speak too quick." She looked up at Dot. "The writing is hard. I read books, not—" she mimicked writing with her right hand.

Dot's face brightened. "I will help you. Many people have handwriting that is hard to read." She took the paper from Rani. "It is from Mr. Thornbridge," she said, glancing at the signature first. "He says he will be here at 11 a.m., and Mr. Martin will come, too."

"It doesn't say they find Krishan?"

"No, miss."

Rani sighed and looked away.

"But I am sure they will!" Dot said. "Do not give up."

"Thank you. I go downstairs to wait."

~

"JOHN COACHMAN MADE good time driving to London," Cecilia observed, looking out the carriage window as they drove into the city environs.

"Not as much traffic this time of year," said James. "And Reuben is good at pacing the horses," he said, using their John Coachman's real name.

"I wonder how far behind are the staff that are joining us in London?"

"They travel in a heavier conveyance that's well laden. You cannot expect them to make the time we did."

Cecilia nodded as she continued to stare out the window. In some ways she missed London, but not in others. She enjoyed their estate and the time she and James had to be together. However, she enjoyed London, too. She was looking forward to enjoying town life for a brief bit of time—so long as Soothcoor's nephew could be found swiftly.

As the carriage turned down the street, Cecilia

reached back to grab James's hand. "I think that is Mr. Thornbridge entering our townhouse. He has another gentleman with him."

James leaned over her to look out the window. "Then I would say our arrival is well timed."

~

"MR. THORNBRIDGE! HO THERE!" David heard from behind him, as Charwood opened the door to the Branstoke townhouse.

"Mr. Martin! Well met! Just in time. I've just arrived myself," David said. They entered the house together. David handed Charwood his beaver hat and the great-coat he'd donned that morning, for the weather was colder.

"I'll keep my coat on, thank you," Lewis told Charwood. "The clothes I have on underneath are not suitable for the parlor of a fashionable house!" he said with a laugh.

David noted the man looked haggard. Most likely up all night. "You have been about the city. Have you discovered anything?" David asked. The door to the parlor opened. "I heard you come in. Have you found Krishan?" Rani asked from the parlor doorway. She squeezed her hands together until her fingers were nigh white.

"Regrettably, not yet," said Lewis slowly. "However, I have news. Shall we adjourn to the parlor to discuss my findings?" he asked. He extended his hand in Rani's direction.

The front door flew open. Rani stood, awed, at the woman, no taller than she, who swept into the room, her hands immediately stripping off pale-blue leather gloves and tossing them on the hallway table.

"Mr. Thornbridge! What is happening? What is

going on at the docks!" demanded the woman, as she burst among them in the hall, a tall gentleman in a multi-caped greatcoat close behind her. The woman looked about the hall. She had the darkest blue eyes Rani had ever seen, and wavy, pale blonde hair, like the angels she'd seen in pictures in church.

"Why didn't you send a note with George? Who are these people?" she demanded as she unbutton her pelisse. She looked at Rani. "Isn't that my dress?" She looked back at David. "What child was kidnapped? And how do you know this? George can be so garbled sometimes. He said something about Soothcoor? We came as fast as we could. Or as fast as James would allow us," she grumbled, as she shrugged out of her pelisse and handed it to Charwood along with her bonnet.

The gentleman laid a hand on her arm. "Cecilia! Easy, my love. Give Mr. Thornbridge a chance," he drawled. He looked around the hall. "It appears as if he and this gentleman have just arrived, as well. And this must be the Indian woman George Romley spoke of." He nodded toward Rani, a slight, reassuring smile on his lips. Rani smiled tentatively back at him, then looked down at the floor.

He took the blonde woman's arm. "Let's adjourn to the parlor so we may hear the tale. Charwood, refreshment, please, and I suggest including something stronger than tea. I believe some will appreciate it," the man said in his calm, urbane manner.

David Thornbridge gave a visible sigh of relief. "Thank you, Sir James. Lady Branstoke, I admit I was deliberately vague with Mr. Romley. But it is as I told him, someone has kidnapped a child off the East India Docks. This is his ayah, Miss Rangaswamy, and this gentleman is Mr. Lewis Martin, from Bow Street. The child is Christopher Sedgewick."

"Yes, yes, Krishan," Rani piped in, stepping further into the hall. "He is only five. And so small. It is my fault. All my fault," she said, tears springing to her eyes.

"Miss Rangaswamy, you are too hard on yourself," put in Lewis. "I have spoken to witnesses. I think it would have happened one way or another."

"Sedgewick, you say. Romley suggested the child has a relationship to the Earl of Soothcoor." James said.

"His nephew," David Thornbridge said heavily. "But how did he know that? I never said the child's name to him."

"I told him," said Charwood, "for I felt that alone made the tale improbable. I told Mr. Romley I fear you are being scammed," he declared, lifting his chin.

"No!" Rani declared, her hands bunching into fists at her side. "I know you not like me because I am Indian, but I speak truth! He is nephew to Earl of Soothcoor!"

"And for that reason, the victim," added Lewis dourly.

"What?" David spun around to stare at Lewis. Rani and Cecilia gave inarticulate sounds of distress. Rani stumbled backward, sagging against the parlor doorframe.

James took in a visibly deep breath. "Let's go into the parlor. I think these events will require some telling. And Charwood," James said, looking at him levelly, "if you feel you have information to contribute, please join us as well."

"I shall get the refreshments," Charwood said, scowling.

Cecilia led the way into the ground floor gold parlor. David solicitously escorted Miss Rangaswamy in.

"She angry I wear her dress," Rani whispered to David.

"No, she's not. She just noticed it."

Rani shook her head. "I should not. I should wear my saree."

"No," David insisted. "You shouldn't. It is too cold in England for your saree. It's colder today than yesterday, too. We will order you some clothes."

She looked up at him doubtfully but compressed her lips and nodded.

David led her to sit on a gold and Egyptian-brown striped damask sofa near the fireplace. He took a chair near her. Lewis did not sit. He stood by the fireplace. The Branstokes sat on the matching sofa across from Rani.

"Who should begin?" asked James. "David?"

"I think Miss Rangaswamy should start, then I will continue and advise on what I have discovered," suggested Lewis.

James noncommittally studied the Bow Street officer, then turned to Rani. "All right. Miss Rangaswamy, if you would, please," he invited.

"Yes, yes," Rani said, in her bright manner. She sat straighter on the sofa, perched on the edge. "Please forgive my English. My uncle, my teacher, would be unhappy. I will try to do better."

"Do not concern yourself with your English, Miss Rangaswamy. You have been under a great deal of stress," James said. "I'm sure speaking in another language would be difficult for anyone under the circumstances."

She nodded. "Thank you, Sir James." She took a breath. "Sahib—Mr. Sedgewick—he write a letter to his brother and say to me to have it delivered when the ship dock. This I do. Sahib say his brother would send people to get us when he gets the letter, but no one come. We wait and wait. Lascars take our things off the ship, and we wait more. No one comes." She looked down at her fingers, twisting together in her lap. She looks up again.

"I decide we cannot wait anymore. I have direction and money from Sahib, but I don't know how to go. I try to get man to talk to me. No one talks. They hurry past," she said, her fingers wiggling to mimic walking away. "I ask another man, and then I hear Krishan yell my name. I turn," she said, turning her body. "A woman is carrying Krishan away. I run, but I fall, and I don't see them when I get up. I look all around, and then I go to our things. No one will help. I don't know what to do. Then Mr. Thornbridge, he comes and helps."

A light knock on the door signaled Charwood returning with refreshments. Rani hesitantly rose to assist Lady Branstoke with serving the tea and savory snacks. Cecilia smiled at her. Charwood returned a moment later with the brandy decanter and glasses from the library. Lady Branstoke waved him over to give her a glass of the stronger beverage.

"How did you come to be at the dock, Mr. Thornbridge?" Cecilia asked, as she set her small brandy glass on the table next to her.

"I check in a few times a week. My intention is for my visits to discourage any new untoward activities," he said frankly.

She nodded. "I thank you for that. Soon that will be unnecessary." She leaned back against the cushions of the matching striped sofa across from Rani. "The company will be sold before year end. The contracts are in the hands of the solicitors right now."

David nodded. "Congratulations. I'm glad to hear it. Under the circumstances, I am glad I was there. A mudlark alerted me to Miss Rangaswamy's plight. Said there was a foreign lady crying on the dock. When I approached, I did not know I would enter *another* mystery. I took her to Bow Street and the Chief Clerk assigned Mr. Martin to assist us."

James and Cecilia looked at the Bow Street officer. He had been listening with his head down, but he raised his head now.

Fatigue etched his good-looking, craggy features, making his blue eyes stand out in his wan complexion.

"Yes. Now it is my turn." He had eschewed the brandy in favor of tea, being too fatigued for any spirits. He set his teacup and saucer on the mantel. "Muriel Patterson is the name of the woman who took young Sedgewick. She is dead."

"What?" came from everyone in the room.

"How?" James uncrossed his legs and leaned forward in his chair.

Martin looked at him, then turned back to address the company at large. "She was stabbed. My witness—"

"Someone saw her get stabbed?" David interrupted.

Lewis Martin nodded. "Nearly. My witness came upon her before she succumbed. She told him two men offered her five pounds to snatch the boy. She knew it was too good to be true. Mrs. Patterson was not in the habit of kidnapping children, or any other larceny, but five pounds is a lot of money in the London stews."

"Poor woman," Cecilia whispered.

"Poor woman! She take my Krishan!" protested Rani.

"Yes, but she didn't have to die," Cecilia said

Rani rose to her feet as her voice rose. "Not die? I kill her if catch her!" she said, moving her hands abruptly down as if breaking a stick in half. "You not know Krishan. Krishan so little, so young, in strange place," she shook her head, her English shattered in her distress. "How she say she would do this for money? I not understand."

"Ladies, please, let's let Mr. Martin talk," said James.

Rani frowned but sat down.

"I appreciate the violence of your feelings, Miss Rangaswamy. I imagine you have been through a great deal in the past 24 hours," James said smoothly. "Remember, we are just learning about these events."

Rani pouted but nodded.

He turned back to Lewis. "Who is this witness?" he asked.

"One of the young mudlarks that frequent that area. His name is Daniel Wrightson; however, he often calls himself Dan Wright."

"Dan was with this woman when she died? How did that come about?" David asked.

"He went looking for the woman and the boy. He knew her slightly and knew the area she was from, so he went looking."

"Why?" James asked.

Lewis Martin ducked his head and rubbed his chin with his right hand before answering. A corner of his mouth kicked up in a self-deprecating smile. "He fancies himself a detective," he said ruefully.

"You trust this young man?" James asked.

"Yes, I do."

"I know him as well," said David. "I'd say he's between ten and twelve years of age. He's the lad who sought me out when he saw Miss Rangaswamy crying."

"Interesting." James said. "Continue, sir," he said, nodding to Lewis.

"From the boy, I got an excellent description of the men, and yes, there were two men involved, not one. And I know the direction they took, as one of the Daniel's mudlark gang followed them."

"And they took Krishan?" Rani asked.

"Yes, they did, but the kidnappers then lost him!" Lewis said in disgust.

"You're saying the men who killed the woman they

paid to grab the boy, subsequently had the boy kidnapped from them?" James said, his brow furrowing, drawing his dark brows together.

Lewis laughed once, mirthlessly. "Yes. Our witness saw them take the boy up the outside staircase of a tavern in the Seven Dials area of the city, lock the boy in, then go back to the tavern to drink. The mudlark who followed the men and the boy came back to the dock area. That's where I met him. He led me and another of my men to the tavern. By the time we got there, the kidnappers had gone back to the room to find the boy missing. They were anxious and asking all around if anyone had seen anything. No one admitted to that, of course. No one ever claims to see anything in that area unless money is involved." He paused and scratched the side of his neck at the edge of the rough wool coat collar.

"We arrested them, and after a little persuasion, and the reminder we had them on the murder of Muriel Patterson, got them to tell us why they kidnapped the boy. They told us they were hired to ensure the boy did not reach the Earl of Soothcoor, by any means."

"Did they ask why?"

"No, and didn't want to know. They were hired about a month ago to loiter around the docks and be on the lookout for a young male child coming from India to England, probably traveling just with his ayah."

"Who hired them?"

"They don't know. They can't even give an appropriate description as the person appeared to be wearing theatrical makeup."

"Shouldn't that, in itself, be a clue?" James asked.

"Perhaps. It is certainly a trail we will follow."

"So what now?"

He looked directly at James. "We begin again," he

admitted. He looked over at Miss Rangaswamy. "It would help if we had a likeness of the child."

"Aah! Yes, yes!" Rani said excitedly, bouncing up off the sofa. "In luggage!"

"You have a painting of the child?"

"Yes, yes! Small, and folded like a book." She mimicked closing a book with her hands.

"A miniature," Lady Branstoke suggested.

Rani nodded. "Yes, miniature."

"Is it a good likeness? One an artist could copy?" Lewis asked.

"Yes!" she nodded vigorously.

"Where is your luggage now?"

"I had it stored at the Waddley Spice and Tea Warehouse at the wharf," David said.

"Excellent, Mr. Thornbridge," said Cecilia. She reached for the bellpull. "Mr. Martin, I see you have not slept. A nap is in order. I shall have Charwood show you to a room where you can sleep."

"That is not necessary, Lady Branstoke."

"I understand that you are a gentleman of the law, Mr. Martin," Cecilia said severely; "however, that does not make you different from any other man. You need your rest. Even a short rest." She stared him down.

"Best to agree, Mr. Martin," said James, laughing.

The door to the parlor opened.

"Charwood, has the Summerworth staff arrived?"

"Yes, madam, and Cook says she will have a cold collation in the dining room whenever you wish."

"Have a footman take Mr. Martin to a guest room to rest, and tell Cook we will have lunch now. Mr. Martin, please go with Charwood."

Lewis exchanged glances with James; however, he followed Charwood out of the room.

"Now, Miss Rangaswamy, we must find you other

clothes to wear, and," she said, looking down at Rani's feet, "shoes."

"I am sorry I wear your dress! Mrs. Dunstan, she say—"

Cecilia waved her hand airily, interrupting her. "Wearing my dress is what I would have expected. But that color does nothing for you. Come, Sarah should have my clothes unpacked by now, and we will find something better suited to you. Afterward, I will have Sarah go out to buy you shoes."

"I have money!" Rani protested.

"Yes, that is good. What we don't have is time," Cecilia said. "All our thoughts and energies need to be centered on finding the boy."

"I need to send word to Soothcoor. As it is, it will take several days for him to get here." James said.

"I sent an express to him first thing this morning," David said, "And I told him I had taken Miss. Rangaswamy to your home and would have the boy brought here, too, when he is found."

"Well done, Mr. Thornbridge," Cecilia enthused, beaming at him.

"Thank you, my lady," David said, bowing.

"Come, Miss Rangaswamy," Cecilia said as she stood up, "let's get you better outfitted. We have much to do this day."

# CHAPTER SEVEN

"Ah, there you are, Mr. Martin." James studied the man as he descended the stairs into the hall, where everyone gathered. "You look better."

His hair was damp. He ran a hand through his blond curls. "I feel better. Thank you, sir, and thank you, Lady Branstoke, for your insistence," he said, bowing in her direction.

Cecilia smiled at the runner as she put her bonnet on her head and tied the ribbons.

"And did you get anything to eat?"

"Yes, my lady, your footman brought me food and a clean shirt and cravat. It is amazing how much better a fellow can feel with an hour's nap and in a clean shirt." His lips twisted into an odd half smile.

"Indeed, it is. I've had occasion to experience that myself," James drawled.

Cecilia exchanged meaningful looks with her husband as they remembered that night in May when they found the stolen government subsidies in the Western Heights tunnels.

"I've had the carriage ordered. With five, we will be tight."

"I shall ride atop with your coachman," said Lewis. "I'm not fond of confined spaces."

James looked at him speculatively but nodded. "Very well. Shall we go?"

In the carriage, Cecilia drew Rani to sit next to her when she would have sat with her back to the driver. Lady Branstoke had Rani dressed in a turkey-red pelisse with a zigzag thunderbolt design woven into the nap of the material. Her bonnet was straw with turkey-red ribbons and bows. On her feet were stout black boots that Sarah had found for her. The dark red looked rich against her darker hair and eyes. When Cecilia and Sarah selected the dress for her, Cecilia mused the vibrant dress and pelisse ensemble would look far better on Rani than they had ever looked on her. She was pleased with how easily and quickly they'd attired her. Luckily, they were similar in size. Tiny!

As Cecilia looked at Rani attired in red, she wondered why she even ordered the outfit for herself. She conceded it was the raised lightning design that caught her attention, and the modiste had done a masterful job of using the design on the bodice panels in contrasting bias directions. Perhaps the same dress and pelisse pattern done up in a pale blue or pink instead?

At the docks, Rani was the last to step down from the carriage. She hesitated before taking Mr. Thornbridge's hand as memories flooded her mind of the day before. The weight returned to her chest, fear rising suddenly, threatening to take over her mind. It was the rising fear that, determinedly, shook her out of the memories. She had no time for fear. She took his hand and stepped down.

At least this day, though colder, was clear and bright. She would take that as an omen for their success.

Only Lewis and James noticed her hesitation and

saw the brief shadow of fear cross her expression before she straightened and smiled at Mr. Thornbridge as he helped her down.

David led them down the crowded dock to the Waddley Spice and Tea Company warehouse. "I had the warehousemen put the luggage on the third floor and told them to mark it for the Earl of Soothcoor," he explained as they approached the office door, away from the coming and going wagons, carts, and sleds near the open double doors. He would have escorted them immediately inside, except James and Lewis paused at the entrance to look around, observing the people on the wharf and their activities.

It was not as wildly crowded as it had been the previous day, but the sounds were much the same—shouting, hammering, screeching rusty hoists, metal-rimmed wheels along the wharf, and the ever-present sound of the lapping water. It was a din that had previously invigorated David Thornbridge. Now he yearned for rural sounds.

Once inside, David led them all to a side staircase, away from the platforms and pulleys used to bring goods to the higher floors. They climbed the narrow side staircase to the third floor. At the third-floor landing, he requested they stay where they were while he talked to the clerk on duty.

He crossed to a battered lectern near the gaping opening in the floor through which screeching pulleys hoisted the goods from below. A young man in a rusty black jacket and checkered waistcoat perched a hip on a high stool by the desk while he wrote in an account book.

"Mr. Comber, where might I find the luggage stored for the Earl of Soothcoor?"

"Oh, hello, Mr. Thornbridge, sir. One moment

please," that worthy said. His ink-stained fingers flipped back a couple of pages in the account book.

*"Hey! Comber! Where's this lot to go?"* yelled a man from across the opening, as he pulled a swinging pallet toward himself.

Comber ignored him as he looked up the information for David. "Northwest corner, aisle two, sir." The man's brow furrowed deeply. "But sir, didn't you come back last night?"

*"Comber!"*

Comber waved his hand at him as he looked at Mr. Thornbridge.

"No. Why do you ask?" David frowned.

The fellow shifted off the stool. "When I come in this morning, I walked the floor, like I always do. Things just looked shifted around.—Oh, not to worry, none of the pieces are missing," he assured David. "I compared the inventory count, and it's the same as when delivered."

The pride in the man's voice kept David from reprimanding him for not notifying him of the disturbance. "Very good," David said shortly. "Thank you."

*"Comber! Get your arse back to da book and tell me where it goes lest I drop it back down the hole!"* yelled the man, as David picked his way back across the floor cluttered with coils of ropes, spare pulleys, and winches.

"Something the matter?" Lewis asked David when he rejoined them.

"I don't know. Possibly." He looked back at the clerk. "He said the luggage has been disturbed, but all pieces are there. It's this way." He led them through a maze of equipment and past crates, barrels, and canvas bags of goods to the northwestern corner of the warehouse where the clerk said they'd stored the luggage.

Lewis dropped into a crouch beside the luggage.

"Miss Rangaswamy, were all these bags and cases locked?"

She walked up beside him. "Just this and this." She pointed to the two larger domed trunks, clad in embossed bare tin, with heavy wood slats along the edges, and leather handles at either end.

He studied the locks on the trunks, his head tilting from side to side as he examined each. "There are marks of tampering on these locks."

"How can you tell?" asked James.

Lewis pointed to the telltale scratches.

"Interesting," Cecilia said, as she, too, peered at the markings. "It looks by the scarceness of marks that the trunks were easy to open, or the effort abandoned."

Lewis laughed mirthlessly. "Oh, they were opened, madam." He pointed to the small scrap of fabric caught in the side. "These locks are not the best quality and they are easily opened. Do you have keys, Miss Rangaswamy?"

"Yes, yes! I have here." Rani rummaged in the reticule Cecilia gave her and handed him two keys tied with a ribbon. "I look in other bags," she said, moving around him to a portmanteau.

"Wait, miss." Lewis reached back to stop her. "I would rather we do this methodically. I would like to see how the contents are before we search through them for what might be missing."

"Oh!" She backed away from the bag she was going to open and clasped her hands together to still her impatience.

Cecilia laid a gloved hand lightly on Rani's forearm. "I know just how you feel! I should be impatient to examine everything."

Rani nodded. "I want to do. Do something."

"In a moment, miss, I will need you to go through

everything," Lewis said as he unlocked the first trunk and lifted the lid.

Rani gave a cry of distress at the jumbled appearance of the trunk's contents. Filled with Krishan's clothes and possessions, someone obviously dug through the trunk, searching for something. On top, spilled across his jumbled clothes, was the contents of Krishan's little treasure box of favorite rocks, toy soldiers, buttons, and other items dear to him.

She instinctually reached for the box, then pulled her hand back before touching it and looked at Lewis.

"Yes, you can go through this trunk now and gather the child's things. I also need you to tell me if anything is missing. I will open the next trunk and other bags," he said.

"I'll help you," Cecilia told Rani.

"What are you thinking someone was looking for?" David asked.

Lewis shrugged as he put the key in the lock of the second trunk.

"Given that someone did not want the child to get to Soothcoor, I'd guess it would be some documentation of the child's legitimacy," James suggested.

"Legitimacy?"

"Yes. If Owen Sedgewick is dead, the child becomes Soothcoor's heir, unless he is his natural son," James explained.

"If Sedgewick was not married to the boy's mother," Lewis clarified.

"Precisely." James crossed his arms over his chest.

"How did you come by that motivation?" David asked.

"It is but one possibility for the kidnapping and luggage search."

"I agree with Sir James," said Lewis. "Something those two men who orchestrated the kidnapping said leads me in that direction." Lewis swore quietly. "The trunk's lock had been forced open, so its key no longer fits easily." Lewis's brows crew together as he struggled with the mechanism.

"What do you mean?" David asked.

"Remember when Mr. Martin told us they were to prevent the child from getting to Lord Soothcoor by any means?" James cut in while Lewis manipulated the stubborn lock. "Any means can include murder, and murder means high stakes. Not much higher than a title and wealthy estate inheritance."

The lock suddenly clicked open, and Lewis lifted the lid.

"Are there other heirs if Sedgewick died without a legal heir?" Lewis asked absently as he looked into the second trunk, also rifled like the first.

"The old Earl was married three times," James said. "Soothcoor is the son of his first wife, a Scottish woman by the name of Adamina; Owen is the son of his second wife, Susan; and by his third wife, Lydia, he had a daughter and three sons, two of whom—twins, and the youngest of the Earl's children—are also currently in India," James explained.

"You know the family well?" Lewis asked, as he picked up a portmanteau to open.

"I know Soothcoor well," James corrected.

"Did you know them? Know Owen Sedgewick's brothers that were in India?" Cecilia asked Rani as she held some articles for her.

"I see them once," Rani said. "They not like Sahib." She stood up and looked at the rest of them. She wrinkled her nose. "They—they party, and—" She made a quick, repeated throwing motion with her hand as she sought for the word she wanted. "And dice?"

"They liked to gamble?" asked James.

"Yes, yes. Gamble with dice. Sahib say they are too young to be in India."

"Miss Rangaswamy, is this the painting you were mentioning?" Lewis asked. He held out a hinged tryptic of paintings in gilt frames.

"Oh! Yes, yes!" she cried. She took the frames from him and opened them. There were three paintings: a man, a woman, and a child.

"See, Sahib, Memsahib, and Krishan."

"This is lovely! I thought it would be a miniature of the boy," Cecilia said.

"An engraver can easily work from this size for an excellent likeness of the child," James observed.

"Look, James, his eyes are so like Soothcoor's," Cecilia said, pointing to the characteristic Soothcoor wide-set and slightly downturned eyes. Puppy eyes.

Tears filled Rani's eyes. She clutched the trio of pictures to her chest. "We must find him!" she said. She bit her lip and tried to stop the tears, but they would flow beyond her will.

Cecilia handed her a handkerchief, put her arm around her and drew her to her. "Oh, my dear, we will. We will."

"My apologies, Miss Rangaswamy, but can you assist me?" Lewis asked. "I need you to go through the rest of these bags with me so we can finish here and get the picture to an engraver."

"Mr. Martin!" David Thornbridge protested for intruding in Rani's sorrow.

Rani sniffed. She wiped her eyes. "Yes, yes. We must finish," she said stoutly, rallying her feelings.

She joined Lewis in going through the rest of the luggage. When they'd finished with the last piece, Rani planted her hands on her hips and stared at the pile of luggage, frowning.

"What is it? What's missing?" Lewis asked.

"The Singing Bird."

"The singing bird? What is that?"

She put her hands together in the shape of an oval. "A box. A silver box. A bird comes out and sings."

"A music box!" said Cecilia.

"Yes. It is Krishan's favorite thing. He loves it even though it does not work anymore. Sahib say his uncle will fix."

"It was packed in one of these bags?" Lewis asked.

"Yes, small bag. Krishan would hold the box when he sleeps at night, so we pack in small bag."

"And that is the only thing missing," stated James.

"Yes."

"What about any papers, documents, that sort of thing?"

"I keep on me," she laid her arm across her waist. "In saree, for safety."

"Where are they now?"

"In my bedroom."

"Someone should immediately examine those," Lewis said. "Miss Rangaswamy, if you would trust me with those pictures, I would take them to an engraver to have Krishan's likeness made."

"Yes, yes!" She kissed the tryptic frame, then handed it to Lewis.

"While you see to that task, Mr. Martin, we shall examine Miss Rangaswamy's papers," James offered.

"I was trusting you would see to that undertaking. If there are names mentioned, you would have a better understanding of the documents. I do not know when I will see you again, as I have to check with my sources. I will also see to acquiring the ship's passenger list and start the queries at the pawnbrokers for a broken silver music box."

"Do not forget to sleep and eat, Mr. Martin," Cecilia admonished.

He flashed her a grin. "I won't, madam, and thank you."

She looked at him with compressed lips and a glint in her eyes that said she didn't believe him but said nothing further.

James tucked his wife's arm in his. "Mr. Thornbridge, please see that Miss Rangaswamy's baggage is transported to my townhouse at the earliest."

"Yes, James. I will remain here to question others to see if they saw or heard anything. I am disturbed that the luggage was touched, and that they did not notify me."

James nodded. "I was about to make the same suggestion. I do not think the men Mr. Martin has arrested had anything to do with the luggage disturbance."

Lewis concurred. "The timing is off."

"Both of you come by later when you can. There will always be food available, a bed to rest in, and clean linens to refresh you," Cecilia told Lewis and David.

"In the meantime, I shall be making some inquiries at my clubs concerning rumors about Soothcoor and his family's relationships."

"I hate it when he does that and learns things I am not privy to," Cecilia grumbled. "Dratted men's clubs."

The gentlemen laughed.

# CHAPTER EIGHT

The ticking of the ormolu mantel clock, the impatient tapping of Lady Branstoke's fingers on the upholstered chair she sat in, and the rustling of papers as James read one document after another were the only sounds in the library.

Rani looked about the room from where she and Lady Branstoke sat in front of his desk and waited for James to finish his review of the documents she had brought from India. The library was a man's domain, with heavy, dark wine-colored drapes at the pair of windows facing the street. The rest of the room's walls were lined with mahogany bookshelves, the books all neatly organized. A thick Persian rug covered most of the floor. Twin reading chairs flanked the fireplace. A sofa sat before it.

James tossed the papers on to his gleaming mahogany desk and looked up. "There is nothing in these papers, Miss Rangaswamy, to show if Owen Sedgewick was married or not. They are primarily about his financial dealings. It appears he did well for himself."

Rani looked dismayed. She stared down at the small pile of papers as she bit her lower lip.

"You are certain they were married?" he asked.

"Yes, yes. Memsahib, she speaks of it, and she smiled when she did." Rani frowned. "Though she said it was a secret from the Company."

James nodded. He leaned back in his chair, crossing his arms over his chest. "I can see that. Over the last decade, the East India Company has frowned on Anglo-Indian mixed marriages."

"Why?" Cecilia asked, her delicate features drawn together in a frown. She picked up the papers to review.

"Because of James Kirkpatrick. He took on the cultural manner, dress, and—some think—the religion of India to the extent that the Duke of Wellington, during his time in India, wondered at the man's loyalty to Britain, and if he, or others like him in their passion for everything Indian, might have compromised loyalties and become spies for India."

"But consorts and natural-born children are allowed?"

"It isn't so much as they are allowed as they are ignored," James said wryly. "And since the Kirkpatrick situation, more British wives have been allowed to accompany their husbands to India. In the last century, a wife accompanying her husband wasn't automatically allowed. It was an arduous process to petition for a family to go to India."

"So, men took Indian women as consorts for companionship," Cecilia concluded.

James nodded.

"And when the consort dies, the children go away," Rani bitterly added.

James and Cecilia looked at her curiously. "What do you mean?" Cecilia asked.

"The man, he loves his woman. Not so much his children. Women die, they send away children. Sent to relatives, sold, sent to an orphanage." She shrugged. "Just so the man did not have to bother with them."

"How awful!" Cecilia exclaimed.

James looked compassionately at her. "This is personal for you."

Rani looked down and nodded.

Cecilia stood up, quivering with indignation, her twilight blue eyes flashing. "James, this cannot be allowed! We must bring this up to Parliament."

"My love, The East India Company has been allowed to make their own laws for over one hundred years. Parliament would not take an interest."

"But that's outrageous!" Cecilia paced behind the chair she'd sat in.

"It is much the same as what happens here in England with a man's mistress," he reminded her. He turned to Rani. "Miss Rangaswamy, if I may ask, do you know who your father is?"

She shook her head. "My uncle, he knows, but I don't ask. My uncle came and got me from an orphanage. He raised me in his family as a daughter. He was a teacher. Many families wanted sons to have a chance to work for the company."

"The East India Company?"

"Yes. Uncle took Christian teachings, and the family converted so the Company would like him more, approve of him as a teacher. He teach English and numbers and science to Indian families who pay him, and later Uncle help them get jobs at the Company."

"It sounds like your uncle was a smart man," James observed.

"Yes, yes. Uncle was very smart. I was happy with family, and I learned, too!"

"How did you come to be a nursemaid for Owen Sedgewick?"

Rani sighed. "When my aunt, she die, my uncle, he

thinks it is punishment from the gods for taking the Christian beliefs so he could make more money. He say he must atone. He sell everything, gave the money to his son, Manoj, and vowed to be an ascetic and wander the country. He said his son, my cousin, would take care of me, but no. Manoj tells me he found a position for me. I must go to work. But these people where he sends me, they are bad people. They beat me! I thought I would die."

Cecilia stopped pacing, her expression full of horror. She grabbed the edge of the high-back upholstered chair she'd sat in, as she leaned forward to listen to Rani.

"I escaped one morning with the clothes I wore. I am Christian, so I go to the English church, and the vicar, Mr. Crane, and his wife, they help me find a position," Rani finished.

"So you were not raised to be a servant, or expected to be one?" James asked.

She shook her head. "No, but it is all right," she said with a shy smile.

"When did all this happen?" Cecilia asked. She came around to the front of the chair and sat down again.

"Five years. Right after Krishan was born. Memsahib was doing poorly, so I come to help and I stay. She, Sushmita Dhar, was beautiful, but she got sick a lot. Finally, she got sick and did not get better. We were all sad."

She tilted her head to the side as she remembered, her brown eyes shadowed with memories. "But that last illness, it was different. Before, it was always in her chest and how she breathes. Last time it was her stomach."

"I wonder if she had asthma," Cecilia mused.

"Yes! That is the word Sahib used," Rani said excitedly.

The clock chimed. James looked up at it. "It is getting late in the day. I wonder if we shall see either gentleman today. I am debating if I should have dinner at the club tonight."

"And have rumors start that we are at outs?" Cecilia teasingly said.

James laughed.

"You may go after dinner—if you must." She compressed her lips, then smiled wryly. "And truthfully, I suppose you must. You men claim women gossip, but I swear you bring home more gossip from the men at the clubs than I do from an afternoon tea with the ladies."

"Sometimes," he conceded.

"I suppose you are going to see what you can learn about Charles Sedgewick."

"Such was my thought."

"It's a good thought. I discussed dinner with Cook earlier today. We are keeping to country hours tonight, so dinner should be in about an hour. I should like to go upstairs to freshen up."

"An excellent idea," James said. He looked over at Rani. "Miss Rangaswamy, might I keep these papers a while longer? There are a few mentions in them I'd like my solicitors to follow up on regarding Owen Sedgewick's London connections for his business."

"Yes, yes, please," she said. She rose from her chair. "I should like to rest before dinner, if that is permitted?" she asked.

"Of course, Miss Rangaswamy! No need to ask. We shall see you then."

CECILIA NESTLED in the corner of a parlor sofa, kicked off her slippers and brought her feet up. It felt odd not to have James here in the evening. Since they wed last

May, they'd scarcely been apart in the evening. They enjoyed their quiet time after supper, talking, reading, or for her, working on her needlework.

She considered herself a competent but hardly a talented needlewoman. What she liked about needlework was it allowed her mind to wander and think of varied things. While the wandering mind hindered the speed of her needlework execution, it did not impede progress. The fichu she edged with white-work embroidery would be done when it was done.

She took a deep breath in, then let it out, feeling tension seep away. It had been a whirlwind day since George arrived at Summerworth Park during breakfast with the news from Mr. Thornbridge. She could not conceive that it had just been that morning! The thought of a child kidnapped wrung her heart, and the knowledge he was the nephew of Soothcoor was particularly upsetting. Soothcoor would cherish his nephew, and it would tear at him that he was not in London for the search.

Soothcoor, with his long face, gray-streaked, straggly black hair, and his dour outward expression, was as much a play actor as she had been with her feigned megrims and palpitations last spring—not that her play-acting ever fooled James.

Few in society knew Soothcoor supported homes and training for young women betrayed by circumstances in their lives. Cecilia smiled as she remembered how gruff Soothcoor became when she discovered his "hobby."

She found it sad that Soothcoor had never discovered love for himself, for he had so much love to offer. It was bottled up inside him, the cork tapped in tightly.

Why would anyone want to kidnap Soothcoor's nephew? From Miss Rangaswamy's description, he was a small child, more delicate than robust. Why would someone expect him to come to England? Curiouser, why would Sedgewick send his son and Miss Rangaswamy to England? From the papers she and James read, the source of Owen's Sedgewick's wealth lay in India. Wouldn't it be better to keep the child where he would be comfortable? From Miss Rangaswamy understanding, the notion to send them away had been spontaneous, yet someone in England clearly expected it. Had some ship arrived from England with a communication that spurred Sedgewick's decision?

Miss Rangaswamy had not mentioned Sedgewick receiving any communication, but would she have known if he had? She believed the drive for them to sail to England had been Sedgewick's health. Miss Rangaswamy said he was dying. Did he suffer apoplexy along with his *arthritis deformans*?

She tied off the white thread for the leaf spray she'd finished at the edge of the fichu, snipped the thread free, then reached into her basket for more white thread to start on the other side of the decorative neck-and-bodice scarf.

She must question Miss Rangaswamy about the nature of Owen Sedgewick's illness. And about ships and messages. Did anyone regularly visit Sedgewick? Might he have received a communication that way?

Ultimately, the only person she could conceive who might benefit from the boy's disappearance would be Charles Sedgewick. Perhaps the solicitors would discover another reason through Owen Sedgewick's business dealings.

Cecilia heard a commotion in the hall and looked up from her needlework as the door to the parlor opened. She smiled. "You're home earlier than I expected!"

James crossed the room, leaned down, and pressed his lips to her cheek. Then he ran his thumb lightly down the side of her face. "The club doesn't hold the fascination for me you do, my love."

Cecilia twisted her lips, though her eye gleamed. "Flatterer. I suppose what your return actually means is Charles Sedgewick is not in town," she drily suggested.

James inclined his head. "True." He crossed to the cut-glass brandy decanter on the sideboard. He held up a glass as he looked at Cecilia. She shook her head. He poured himself a glass, then sat down in one of the wing chairs by the fireplace.

"Where is Miss Rangaswamy?" he asked, looking about the room.

"She retired early. So, what have you learned?" Cecilia pressed, as she picked up her needlework again.

He leaned back, crossing one leg over the other. "Charles has outrun the constable. He traveled north with Soothcoor to rusticate until quarter day."

Cecilia's shoulders shook in silent laughter. "When did he leave?"

"Two weeks ago." James sipped his brandy. "When Soothcoor went north, Sedgewick decided it would be advantageous to travel in his brother's company."

"Cheaper, you mean."

James held up his glass and dipped his head in agreement.

"He could still be responsible for hiring those men. Didn't Mr. Martin say whoever hired the kidnappers did so more than a month ago?"

"Yes, but I am not thinking of the hiring. I am wondering who searched the travel trunks."

"Oh! I see what you mean." Cecilia tilted her head. "Does he have an associate, or are we looking for someone else?"

"The only other person who I can think might want to prevent the child from inheriting is Soothcoor's stepmother, the Dowager Countess."

"I don't recall ever meeting her. Do you know her?" Cecilia asked.

"Yes, and while she would want her son to inherit, and has said so frequently since Owen went to India, she is not the type to plan to do away with a child." He uncrossed his legs and leaned forward, his elbows on his knees, the brandy glass held loosely in his hands. "From what Mr. Martin said, I don't gather this was a kidnapping for ransom. We need to think differently."

At a knock on the parlor door, James straightened and looked up.

"Excuse me, Sir James, madam, but Mr. Martin is here with a young street person," Charwood loftily stated from the doorway.

James glanced at the clock. It was almost ten p.m.

He looked back at Charwood. "By all means, show them in."

"And stay a moment after you show them in, so I may find out if they need anything in the way of food or drink," Cecilia added.

"Yes, madam." Charwood bowed himself out, his posture eloquent with his disapproval.

Cecilia set aside her embroidery and leaned down to tuck her sewing basket under the rosewood table beside the gold-and-brown striped sofa where she sat. "I hope he has good news," she murmured to her husband.

"As do I."

"Mr. Martin and Mr. Wrightson, to see you," Charwood announced.

A red-headed boy in a plaid cap grinned cheekily up at Charwood. Lewis tapped him on the shoulder. "Take your hat off," Lewis admonished. The boy snatched the hat off and held it before him.

Lewis looked over at the Branstokes. "My apologies for the late hour. We won't take up much of your time."

"Come in, please, and sit down. Can we get you anything to eat or drink?" Cecilia asked.

The boy, a gleam in his eyes, swaggered forward. Lewis grabbed his shoulder to pull him back. The boy grimaced up at Lewis. The Bow Street agent didn't look at him. "No, thank you, my lady. I came to return the pictures to Miss Rangaswamy. The fliers will be available in the morning. Daniel, here, will bring them to you while we distribute others in the city. I wanted him to meet you, so he doesn't get turned away at the door," he said, looking meaningfully over his shoulder at Charwood.

Charwood glowered back at him.

"Daniel will serve as my messenger should I need to get news to you and for you to communicate with me. I have told him you have an excellent cook, by way of inducement," he said drily.

James laughed.

"And he shall receive the best of our cook's fare," Cecilia promised, smiling.

"Thank you." He inclined his head. "Now for my news. It is not the best; however, it is news. We believe the boy has been sold to a chimney sweep."

"A chimney sweep!" the Branstokes exclaimed.

"I would not have considered that," James admitted.

Lewis nodded. "Based on Miss Rangaswamy's description, he would be the perfect size for a sweep's apprentice."

"What makes you believe he is now in the hands of a chimney sweep?" James asked.

"It's wot mi gang say," spoke up the boy. He threw his shoulders back, standing tall. "Lil' Eddie hurd it fum Stewie over by Seven Dials. He tol' Ferdie who tol' me."

James looked at Lewis. "You believe this?"

"Yes, I do. Unfortunately, all we have for a description is the approximate height and build of the sweep and the person who sold the child. It was dark, and they both wore dark clothes."

"Is there anything we can do to help? It is vexatious to feel useless," Cecilia said.

Lewis shrugged. "Continue talking to Miss Rangaswamy and see if she remembers anything more that happened around her."

Cecilia nodded thoughtfully. "Yes," she said slowly, a faraway look in her eyes. She looked again at Lewis. "And I can share the flyers with my acquaintances who are still in town and suggest they get their chimneys swept. It is that time of year."

Lewis laughed. "It is, but most of society has nothing to do with the sweeps. It is their servants who do."

Cecilia frowned thoughtfully. "Charwood, when was the last time we had these chimneys swept, and who arranged it?"

"Last spring, madam. Mrs. Dunstan arranges all household matters like cleaning the chimneys," he stiffly admitted.

"Lewis, I shall speak to Mrs. Dunstan, and we will pass the word among her network of housekeepers." Cecilia stood up and paced.

James leaned back in his chair. "Mr. Martin, you have roused my tigress."

Cecilia cast a glance at her husband but continued. "And despite chimney cleaning being the responsibility of the staff, I know it will delight some of my lady friends to be involved. We shall have the cleanest chimneys in England, and we shall find Christopher! It only wants getting the word out, and I believe I know how to do that."

# CHAPTER NINE

*I*n the morning, Cecilia found Miss Rangaswamy in the parlor, the hinged gilt tryptic frame open in her lap.

"Good, you've found your frame. Mr. Martin brought it back last night after you'd retired for the night."

"Yes, yes. I was tired, but I did not sleep," Rani said. Fatigue grayed her complexion and echoed in her voice.

Cecilia crossed the room to sit by her side. "It is not to be wondered. You are sick with worry for your little Krishan, though you have stood up to everything with commendable fortitude."

Rani shook her head, and when she looked up, her eyes glistened with tears. "I think over and over in my head how it might have been different."

Cecilia patted her hand. "Such thoughts are useless. We must move on from where we are. And didn't Mr. Martin say that the kidnapping would have happened one way or another? If events occurred in another manner, you might have been injured, or worse."

"You think this is true?" Rani asked.

"I know it is true," Cecilia countered. "I forget you

weren't there to talk to Mr. Martin last night. He believes Soothcoor's nephew has been sold as an apprentice to a chimney sweep."

Rani wrinkled her nose, and her brow furrowed. She tilted her head. "A chimney sweep? What is this?"

"A man who cleans chimneys. In the city, we use more coal for heat, and coal creates a mess in the chimneys. They need to be cleaned to prevent fires."

"And this chimney sweep, he cleans the chimneys to prevent fires?"

"Yes, but in the city, the chimneys are not straight, and they narrow above the fireplaces, so the chimney sweep takes on boys as apprentices to help him clean the chimneys. They are called climbing boys, as they climb the chimneys and work their way through the maze of chimney flues to clean them."

Rani shook her head. "Krishan would not like to do that work. He would be afraid."

Cecilia sighed. "Most boys are. The sweep has ways to force them up the chimney, and sometimes he lights a fire under them to keep them going."

"No!" "Rani's face paled. "And Mr. Martin, he thinks Krishan has been sold to this chimney sweep? How does he know this?"

"Remember the young boy who sent Mr. Thornbridge to you?"

"Yes."

"Mr. Martin recruits boys like him to be on the watch and listen to what goes on around them. Men don't pay attention to a child in the area."

"Oh, like Mr. Thornbridge and Mrs. Dunstan tell me when you pretend to be sick."

Cecilia laughed. "Yes, it is the same with children and sickly, whining woman. Men don't pay attention to them. One of Mr. Martin's recruits saw the transaction. He only paid attention when he heard the child speak, as his voice and accent were different. He said the boy tried to fight and run away, but they tethered him to the man selling him and then to the chimney sweep."

"Sahib say slaves are not allowed in England."

"Yes, this is true," Cecilia said. "However, the exchange of money for a child to be taken into an apprenticeship is common. It is not considered the same as slavery. An apprenticeship contract generally runs for seven years, and it is thought to provide the child with a useful trade. But it is not a safe trade, and many climbing boys get stuck in chimneys, fall down a chimney, or have some other horror occur to them."

Rani wrung her hands together and visibly shuddered.

Cecilia lay a hand over Rani's. "We will find him. I have a plan."

Rani looked up at her. "How?"

"I learned last night that it is typically the housekeepers or the butlers that arrange for chimneys to be cleaned. Through the good offices of Mrs. Dunstan and Mr. Charwood, we will recruit the upper servants in London to arrange for chimneys to be swept. It is a good time to do so with many families away for the holidays. They will be given flyers with the picture of Krishan so they can identify him. Those flyers will be here soon. And James and I are offering a five-hundred-pound reward for finding Krishan."

"That is great wealth!" Rani said, her eyes wide.

"Yes. It might even entice the chimney sweep who has Krishan to claim the reward if he learns of it. Mr. Martin's network is spreading the word."

"Excuse me, madam, the flyers are here," said Charwood from the parlor door.

"Excellent!" Cecilia exclaimed, rising from the sofa. "Please bring them in." She pointed to the side table as she walked toward it. "I should like to see them. Did the boy bring them?"

"Yes, madam, he is in the kitchen stuffing his stomach under the watchful eye of Cook." Charwood set the wrapped and string-tied package on the table.

"Good. Tell Cook to make him a basket of food to take with him to share with his fellows."

"Immediately, madam." Charwood bowed and turned to leave.

"Oh, and tell Mrs. Dunstan to join Miss Rangaswamy and me here."

Charwood paused, his back stiff. Then, "Yes, madam," he said, continuing out of the room.

Cecilia stared after him and frowned. Charwood was acting quite peculiar. She turned back to the bundle. "Miss Rangaswamy, would you kindly bring me my sewing scissors?"

Miss Rangaswamy bounced up off the sofa. "Yes, yes!" She grabbed Cecilia's scissors and hurried to her side.

"Thank you." Cecilia cut the knot binding the package and spread the paper covering out.

"Oh, that is Krishan!" Miss Rangaswamy exclaimed.

Cecilia laughed. "Well, it is meant to be! I'm gratified to hear you think it is an appropriate representative likeness."

"His hair is a little longer now, but that is my Krishan."

Cecilia picked up the top flyer. "It does identify him as the Earl of Soothcoor's nephew, so that is good. It directs people who have information to contact Mr. Lewis Martin at Bow Street. I wish it had included us in the notification, or as an alternate, but I supposed Mr. Martin knows what he is doing." She sighed and looked at Miss Rangaswamy. "Now we need to get this out and about."

Mrs. Dunstan entered the parlor. "You asked for me, madam?"

"Yes, and you have come just in time. Come look at these." Cecilia held out a flyer for her housekeeper.

"Well, mercy if he don't have Lord Soothcoor's eyes!" Mrs. Dunstan exclaimed.

"My thought as well when I first saw his picture. Do you think you could share these with your domestic associates? I think you told me once that on days off you like to go to The Pheasant House and gossip with your friends."

Mrs. Dunstan clasped her hands together in front of her and stood up straighter, "Madam, we do not gossip. We exchange experiences," she said, her lips pursed primly.

Cecilia repressed a smile. "Of course, you do. Regardless, what I want is for you to take some to The Pheasant House and pass them out. Tell them Bow Street believes the kidnappers have apprenticed the boy to a chimney sweep, and pass the word that Sir James and Lady Branstoke are offering five hundred pounds for any information that leads to the rescue of Krishan."

Mrs. Dunstan's eyes widened. "Five hundred pounds?"

"Yes. Encourage everyone to hire a sweep to clean their master's chimneys, and to be on the lookout for this boy as a climbing boy. If they think the boy in their chimney is him, they must send word to us immediately! Is that clear?

"This is your most important task. And make sure our servants are aware as well, and give them flyers to pass among their associates. If one of our own is responsible for passing the word on to someone who finds the boy, they shall receive a reward of one hundred pounds."

Mrs. Dunstan blinked. "That is too much, my lady! You will not get a lick of work out of them. They shall be so busy spreading the word."

"Mrs. Dunstan, that is a small price for us to pay in our efforts to find the child." Cecilia picked up the majority of the flyers and handed them to her housekeeper.

Mrs. Dunstan took them and bobbed a curtsy. "Yes, madam. I'll go now."

~

"Lady Oakley, madam," intoned Charwood. He stepped aside to allow Lady Oakley to enter.

Cecilia rose from the parlor sofa to greet her guest. "Lady Oakley, thank you for coming," she said, clasping her guest's hands between hers.

"How could I stay away? Your note was all so mysterious," the lady tittered like a young miss, her brown eyes owlishly wide open behind the lenses of her gold wire-frame glasses.

Cecilia giggled, "Yes, I daresay it was."

Lady Oakley tilted her head to study Cecilia, sending the ostrich feather plumes attached to her purple turban swaying. "You are looking well, my dear. Though I am dismayed to note you are not increasing yet. Or are you?" she bluntly asked. Her thin, pale brows pulled together and her lips pursed as she studied Cecilia.

Cecilia compressed her lips together to keep from laughing. From anyone else in society such a question would be the height of rudeness. Coming from Lady Oakley it was expected.

"No, sadly, not yet," Cecilia answered. "But come, I should like to introduce you to my new friend, Miss Rangaswamy."

Miss Rangaswamy rose from her seat and bobbed a curtsey.

Lady Oakley jutted her narrow chin forward as she studied her. "You're Indian."

"Yes, my lady," Miss Rangaswamy said softly.

"And she had quite the adventure since arriving in London two days ago. We have a mystery, and I am hoping you can help us solve it."

Lady Oakley brightened. "Sounds fun. Please tell me."

"In just a moment," Cecilia said. "Let's all get settled, and we'll have tea while we tell you particulars. It is so vexatious!" she said, as she rang the bell. After she'd requested tea brought in, she led her guest and Miss Rangaswamy to a small, cloth-covered round table at the right of the fireplace where four brown-velvet-covered Chippendale chairs were placed.

"Oh, this is lovely," Lady Oakley said. "Much nicer than trying to speak to one another spread out, as we must be in the center of the room in sofas and chairs."

"My thoughts, precisely," said Cecilia. "Now, you know the Earl of Soothcoor."

"Alastair Sedgewick? Since he was a baby, not that he would ever want to admit he was one. So dour he's become in his middle years," Lady Oakley said, pursing her lips as she frowned.

"And Alastair is his first name? All I've ever known him as is Soothcoor, though I knew Sedgewick was his family name."

"Yes, he was named after his Scots grandfather. His mother was Scottish, you know."

"No, I didn't."

"Yes, indeed. But proceed, now that we have established I know him—and his family."

"Then you know his half-brother Owen went to India some seven years ago."

"It distressed his father, though everyone knew London weather aggravated his condition."

"His *arthritis deformans*. Yes, and I understand from Miss Rangaswamy that he was doing well with only occasional terrible, painful spells. Aside from the weather, they have some medicines in India that did much to ease his suffering."

"Yes, yes!" Rani said. "Some days you would not know he has the illness—" She paused, then admitted, "—unless you look at his fingers, for they are crooked." She held her hands up, positioning her fingers in crooked angles to each other.

"And how do you know Owen Sedgewick, Miss Rangaswamy," Lady Oakley asked, looking over the rim of her teacup.

"I—"

"Miss Rangaswamy was a close friend of his wife, who died a year ago. Now it appears Owen is dying, and he asked Miss Rangaswamy to bring his son to England."

"Son!"

"Yes, he has a five-year-old son, Christopher Sedgewick, with his wife..." Cecilia looked at Miss Rangaswamy.

"Sushmita. Sushmita Dhar."

"And you were close to this Sushmita Dhar?"

"Yes, yes! And she trust her son to me."

"Do you have family in India, Miss Rangaswamy?"

She looked down. "My uncle, who raised me, has taken a vow of poverty. He is an ascetic and roams India."

"How odd," Lady Oakley said. "But one shouldn't judge another culture by ours, or they should judge us and find us wanting, isn't that correct, Cecilia?"

"That is what I believe," Cecilia said.

"So again, we have strayed. What is the mystery?"

"Someone paid others to kidnap little Christopher."

"What!" Lady Oakley exclaimed. She set her teacup down abruptly. Tea sloshed across the tablecloth.

Cecilia used her serviette to blot up the puddle of tea.

"Bow Street believes the miscreants were hired months ago to lie in wait for a ship bringing Christopher Sedgewick to England. Their instructions were to keep him away from his uncle by any means."

"Any means? And how is this known?"

"They captured the men; however, they had lost Christopher before they were captured."

"Lost you say?"

"Yes. Someone kidnapped the child from them!"

"Dear Lord."

"But Bow Street does have a lead. They believe the boy was sold to a chimney sweep as an apprentice."

"A *chimney sweep?*"

"Yes."

"Krishan—Christopher—is five, but he is small. Mr. Martin says he is the size the chimney sweeps want to climb the chimneys." explained Miss Rangaswamy.

"Who is Mr. Martin?"

"Mr. Martin is the Bow Street agent assigned to the case," Cecilia explained.

Lady Oakley frowned. "And what would you have of me? You obviously did not invite me here just to gossip."

Cecilia smiled. "I am hoping to use your connections to spread the word about Christopher and encourage the *ton* to have their chimneys cleaned and be on the lookout for the child."

"Do you have a picture?"

"Better—we have flyers." Cecilia crossed to the sofa where she'd sat before and pulled a stack of flyers from her sewing basket. She laid them before Lady Oakley.

"This is the child?"

Rani nodded.

"Good God, he has Alastair's drooping eyes, poor child."

Rani bristled. "He is a beautiful child!"

The corner of Lady Oakley's mouth kicked up in a half smile. "Yes, he is, but those eyes on an adult male do not carry the same charm as they do on a child. No matter. He is obviously a Sedgewick." She stared down at the flyer picture a moment longer. "Lady Amblethorpe is still in town and has planned a holiday musicale at her home this evening. Anyone remaining in town should be there. You should go."

"We have not been invited."

Lady Oakley slid her a sideways glance. "You will be. And so I must go. I will set my housekeeper to ordering my chimneys swept and pay a little visit on Lady Amblethorpe. If the boy is in London, he will be found. Who could miss those eyes!" She rose from the table. "She looked down at Miss Rangaswamy. "I wish you well, my dear, in whatever you do." She said cagily.

She kissed Cecilia's cheek goodbye and left.

"What did she mean, she wish me well? Her voice was not nice."

Cecilia laughed. "I don't believe it was that she was not being nice. She was telling us she knew Owen Sedgewick employed you, and not a close friend of his wife."

"I was her friend."

"I know. And a good friend," Cecilia said quietly.

# CHAPTER TEN

James arrived home shortly before dinner with Mr. Thornbridge and the Amblethorpe invitation to their Holiday musicale.

"I met the Amblethorpe footman as we were about to mount the steps before the house," he explained to Cecilia, as he handed her the invitation and the note from Lady Amblethorpe apologizing for the late invitation as she did not know they were in town.

"Lady Oakley suggested we go this evening."

"Lady Oakley? When did you have occasion to see her?"

"I invited her for tea. I told her about the child. She will do her part to spread the word, and you know she has a wide circle of acquaintances, not all of whom are part of society."

"Yes, she's a patroness to many otherwise starving artists and artisans."

"And their circles extend outward."

"But why did she think we should go to the Amblethorpe musicales? Not because she knows we met at one of Lady Amblethorpe's musical entertainments, I trust."

Cecilia laughed. "No. She believes all the *ton* who

remain in London will be at the musicale, and it will be an opportunity to spread the word."

"Do you wish to go?"

"Yes, I think we should. How was your day with Mr. Thornbridge?"

"Enlightening. The gentlemen responsible for Krishan's kidnapping have been seen loitering around the docks since early October. They have been there so much—and obviously with no employment or other reason to be there—that the Thames Marine Police have been watching them.

"What is unfortunate is the officer Miss Rangaswamy and I spoke with did not think to connect the men he had been observing over the last month with the kidnapping of the boy, particularly as the actual kidnapper was a woman.

"He saw them not long after Miss Rangaswamy and Mr. Thornbridge had talked to him. They were moving quickly off the wharf, far quicker than he typically saw them move, which is why he noted them."

"I cannot believe we could have possibly resolved the kidnapping issue if the officer had connected the men with Mrs. Patterson," David lamented.

"And what about the warehouse break-in?" Cecilia asked.

"There was a man in the area, perhaps in his forties or fifties, based on witnesses' descriptions. Dressed like a man who would work in the city—neat, subdued, and professional. He stood out for that reason. And he walked about as if he had every right to be there. That is how he was able to enter Waddley's."

"The night clerk is young, and Waddley's is his first position since coming out of school. He was afraid to stop the man, as he looked so comfortable with where he was. He even let him study the account book, which is how he discovered where the Sedgewick luggage could be found."

Cecilia closed her eyes briefly as she shook her head. "Thankfully, the company will soon no longer be our concern. Assign him to days with a senior clerk for at least the next two weeks."

David laughed. "Mr. Smith makes up the schedule, and I told him to assign the man to days for the next three weeks."

Cecilia nodded. "Well done. I don't know why I felt I had to make a recommendation. I should have known you would have had it well in hand."

He inclined his head. "Where is Miss Rangaswamy?"

"She went off with Mrs. Dunstan when she came back for more flyers. She didn't like sitting here and just waiting for news. But I expect them to return shortly."

"I don't blame her for her restlessness," said James.

"When Mrs. Dunstan came back, enthused with the response she'd received from her peers, Miss Rangaswamy's eyes gleamed with excitement. It was the happiest I've seen her since we met. It is good for her to get out."

"Yes, I believe that would put her in good humor. I look forward to seeing her at dinner with her renewed good cheer," said Mr. Thornbridge.

Cecilia and James exchanged glances.

"As do we all," said Cecilia. "Excuse me, I need to freshen up before dinner."

"Mr. Thornbridge, would you care to join me in my library for a drink?" James extended his hand in the direction of his library.

"I should be honored," David said.

~

"HAS Mr. Thornbridge displayed any partiality for Miss Rangaswamy to you?" Cecilia asked her husband, as their carriage took them to the Amblethorpe London townhouse.

"You caught his interest in her when we talked before dinner."

"It was rather obvious. And at dinner he hung on every word Miss Rangaswamy made, as if they were pearls cast before him."

"Yes. He has spoken to me of his admiration for Miss Rangaswamy."

"Admiration?"

"Eloquently," James said dryly.

"Oh dear."

James laughed. "Why do you say *'oh, dear'* in just that tone of voice?"

"I do hope he is not developing a tendre for her."

"Why is that?"

"Mr. Thornbridge has lost all taste for the city, and yearns to return to the country," Cecilia said.

"Yes, we have discussed this."

"Miss Rangaswamy, on the other hand, loves the city. I do not think she would be happy in the country."

"But shouldn't we let them discover this for themselves? Without interference? Have you thought perhaps he may stay in the city for her, or she go to the country for him?"

"I suppose. It's just—Gracious! There is a line of carriages, James! Look!"

James leaned across her to look out her side of the carriage windows. "I would have thought more people would have left London for the holidays by now."

"It will be a crush. Lady Amblethorpe must be thrilled. And she doesn't even have a daughter on the marriage mart."

"We shall have to work diligently with this crowd to

talk up the situation about Soothcoor's nephew and encourage hiring chimney sweeps. "

"Yes." Cecilia stared at the line of coaches. It appeared to be moving with some modicum of steady, albeit slow rate.

"Since perforce we must wait our turn, what had you been about to say regarding Miss Rangaswamy and Mr. Thornbridge?"

She shrugged her slender shoulders. "I've come to care for both of them. They are good people and deserve happiness."

"I'm sure they will find their way," James said.

"Perhaps, but I've sensed Mr. Thornbridge's dissatisfaction with his life."

"We will assist him in finding the right position so he can be content. That is the most we should do. Do not think to get involved with his love life as well. It will not serve, Cecilia," James warned.

She sighed. "Can I help it if I want others to find the happiness we have found together?"

He laughed softly as he pulled her closer to him to kiss her head.

"James! Please, you will disturb all of Sarah's efforts to tame my hair."

"Be careful what you say, madam. I may take that as a challenge." He reached up as if he would pluck a hairpin from her hair.

Cecilia pulled back. "James, no!"

He dropped his hand to her shoulder and squeezed her against him. "Sometimes it is fun to tease you."

"Hmph, and some people consider you the dry, urbane gentleman. At least I have never made that mistake."

Laughter rumbled deep in his chest.

Their carriage finally drew up before the townhouse, and an Amblethorpe footman hurried to open their carriage door and let down the steps. As the footman handed her down, Cecilia looked down the street. There remained a line of carriages behind theirs—as many as had been before theirs—all waiting to discharge their passengers at the Amblethorpe party.

She tucked her arm in her husband's as they climbed the stairs to the brilliantly lit house, the footman running ahead of them to open the door and usher them in before he attended to the next carriage in the line.

"That footman will be exhausted by the time the night is over," Cecilia softly observed.

"For a ball, they would have two. I doubt the household expected this many to attend a musicale. I don't recall the invitation mentioning the entertainment, other than an evening of seasonal music."

"We shall know shortly. There is a woman standing with Lord and Lady Amblethorpe in the receiving line. She looks familiar."

James looked toward their host. "It is Mrs. Billington, I believe."

"I thought she retired."

"She did. It has been about five years or so. However they enticed her to sing tonight, it will be an improvement over the concert where we met."

Cecilia laughed softly. "I am convinced it can't be any worse."

"Now that is surprising," James said.

"What?"

"Lady Soothcoor is here. The Dowager Countess of Soothcoor."

"Soothcoor's stepmother?"

"The same. She has a house in Richmond; however, typically she goes north and spends the holidays at Coor Castle."

"Please point her out to me. I should like to meet her. We should speak to her about Krishan."

James looked down at her. "You call him Krishan as Miss Rangaswamy does. You'll need to remember to call him Christopher to others."

"True. But where is she?"

"See the flame-haired woman by the staircase?"

"That is Lady Soothcoor?"

"Yes. Lady Lydia Soothcoor."

Cecilia studied her. Tall and strong-featured, the woman carried herself with considerable assurance and grace. And she appeared to know everyone. Attired in a deep Nile-green silk gown, she stood with her arm through that of a gentleman a little younger, but fit, confident—and haughty, Cecilia decided, judging by the way the man couldn't seem to get his nose down out of the air to look at anyone directly.

Cecilia tipped her head toward her husband. "Do you know her escort?"

"No. And don't stare. We are almost to the Am-blethorpes."

"A receiving line at a musicale evening is quite out of the norm."

"I'm sure it is for the coup of having Mrs. Billington for entertainment," James said.

"Sir James, Lady Branstoke, I am so glad you could make our musicale, and I am so dismayed at not knowing you were in town to have sent it earlier."

"We only arrived yesterday. When Lady Oakley said she would tell you we were in town, I hardly expected you to extend an invitation at such a late time," Cecilia said.

"Did you know Cecilia and I met at your spring musicale?"

"You met at our musicale? I had no idea," said Lady Amblethorpe.

"Yes," Cecilia said. "And that is why we are delighted to be here tonight."

"Gracious! Then we are honored. It was such a surprise to the *ton* when you married. You are well now?" Lady Amblethorpe asked, for last spring, to all of society, Cecilia had appeared as a woman of fragile health, always with one health complaint or another. Ill health was the ruse Cecilia used to encourage others to ignore her presence and talk openly around her, certain she wasn't attending, so involved she appeared in her own health.

"But please, you must meet our guest of honor, Mrs. Elizabeth Billington!" Lady Amblethorpe enthused.

James bowed over the singer's hand. Mrs. Billington was a stout woman with a hawk nose and a mass of frizzy curls. Hers was a beautiful voice, though some decried a lack of emoting in her singing. Nonetheless, she'd ruled the Vocal Concerts for many years until her retirement in 1810. "My wife and I are looking forward to your performance, madam. You have been away from the stage for far too long."

The woman smiled slightly and acknowledged his comment with a slight nod but otherwise appeared bored. Cecilia and James shared covert glances before continuing to the staircase leading to the ballroom set up for the musicale.

The room looked much as it had at the spring musicale, with rows of Gillows of Lancaster mahogany chairs for seating. Though this time it was not as profusely decorated with flowers, nor as heavily perfumed—understandable, owing to the time of year. The grand ballroom was white with ornately carved and gilded moldings, large-framed mirrors hung every ten feet, and painted murals on the ceiling.

Few of the guests were seated yet, most preferring to mingle and whisper to each other as they awaited the Amblethorpes and their guest, Mrs. Billington. A small ensemble of musicians gathered at the back of the room, murmuring amongst themselves as they sorted their music.

James led Cecilia to where Lady Soothcoor stood with her escort.

"Sir James," Lady Soothcoor said warmly as they approached.

"Lady Soothcoor, I am happy to see you," said James, taking the lady's hand and bowing over it. "I would like you to meet my wife, Cecilia."

"Delighted," the woman said.

Cecilia curtsied slightly, acknowledging the woman's rank.

"Do you know Dr. Jonathan Lakewood?" the Dowager Countess asked.

"I have not had the pleasure," James said, tipping his head toward the gentleman.

"Pleasure," the man responded back to them.

"I knew Dr. Lakewood nine years ago, when he attended my daughter Anne after the difficult birth she had with George. Since then he has become quite famous for his study of the medicinal properties of exotic plants." There was warmth and pride in the Countess's voice.

"What made you develop an interest in exotic plants?" James asked.

"I spent five years in India as a physician with the East India Company and learned about the plants there that are used in Ayurvedic medicine. In fact, it was Lady Soothcoor's stepson who sparked my interest in Ayurvedic medicine and the plants used."

"How is that?" Cecilia asked.

"I had some prior acquaintance with Mr. Sedgewick, as I had met him when I treated Lady Anne. He was much troubled by *arthritis deformans* at that time and was making plans to sail to India for work and relief. When I met him again in India, the good health he enjoyed shocked me. Delightfully shocked. While his hands showed evidence of the disease, he did not seem to be bothered by it. He told me that was because of the local medicine he took. This sparked my interest."

"Dr. Lakewood brought back many different plant seeds, rhizomes, and tubers for further study. I have lent him the use of my conservatory until he can get a proper scientific facility built."

"How wonderful, and quite generous of you, Lady Soothcoor!" Cecilia exclaimed.

"Well, I love exotic plants, so it is for my benefit as well. He has one plant in particular I am in love with, the *Gloriosa Superba*. It looks like a candle flame when it blooms."

"And it is the plant that was the most beneficial for Mr. Sedgewick's affliction."

"I regret to tell you that by this time Mr. Sedgewick may well be deceased," Cecilia sadly disclosed.

"What?" Lady Soothcoor looked sharply at Cecilia.

"He sent his son and his son's nursemaid to England to Soothcoor, as the doctor in India said he had not much time left to live."

Lady Soothcoor smiled and shook her head. "I am sure you are mistaken in your information. Owen swore he would never get married or have a family as he did not want to pass on his affliction to a child. His mother had the same disease, and the poor woman killed herself when she could no longer accept the pain in her life."

"I didn't know Owen's mother took her own life," James said.

"Well, it is not generally discussed, but because he had the disease from his mother, Owen swore he would never pass it on. My son Charles will be the Earl of Soothcoor after Alastair, as Alastair has shown no interest in marriage," Lady Soothcoor said complacently.

"My dear lady, I can confirm Sir James's assertion as to a child. I saw the child. Owen referred to him as Kit," said Dr. Lakewood. "I thought you knew."

"If that is true, which I doubt, he would not be legitimate."

"I have seen a painting of the child. He has the Sedgewick eyes."

Dr. Lakewood thought for a moment, then nodded, "Yes, he did."

Lady Soothcoor frowned.

"Did?" queried Cecilia.

Dr. Lakewood laughed. "As I assume he still does. Eyes' shape and slant don't change, do they?"

"The child was kidnapped two days ago, and Bow Street believes he was sold as an apprentice to a chimney sweep," James said.

Dr. Lakewood's chin came down as he frowned. "Extraordinary," he said.

"Well, at least he has an occupation and will not batten upon society," said Lady Soothcoor.

Cecilia frowned. "Lady Soothcoor, the child is a member of your family," she protested. "Surely you don't wish a member of your family to be a chimney sweep."

"Not my family, and he is a by-blow; he's no concern of mine."

"But he is of concern to your late husband's family," Cecilia pressed.

She laughed. "Oh, I hardly think so. I know I may appear heartless; however, we must face facts, Lady Branstoke."

"The nursemaid tells us Mr. Sedgewick was married to the child's mother," James said.

"No, that is not true. I have it from my twins, who are now in India, that Owen is not married. Marriage with a native is frowned upon by the East India Company, and though I may have had my disappointments in Owen, he has never been a man to ignore the dictates of those above him. He would be too afraid to."

"Miss Rangaswamy, Christopher's nursemaid, has said they kept it secret."

"I should think my sons would know more of their half-brother's affairs than a servant," Lady Soothcoor said pointedly.

James could discern by the tenseness he felt in Cecilia's arm tucked into his that his wife was seething, and if provoked any further, might say something that would not do their plans for the evening good.

"Lady Soothcoor, I am surprised to see you in town. It is my understanding that you typically go north every year for the holidays."

"I did. I traveled north for the sake of my daughter, Anne, and her family. She married Sir Henry Brickston, who had an estate near Coor Castle, you know. Unfortunately, he died last spring in a hunting accident. I convinced Anne to bring the children to London for the holidays. Being in mourning over the holidays at Brickston Hall could not be healthy for the children."

"Our condolences to your family. Do they stay with you in Richmond?"

Lady Soothcoor shook her head. "Alas, no, though I tried to convince her to do so. They have a townhouse in London."

"It looks like people are taking their seats, James. Perhaps we should as well.," Cecilia said, extending her meaning to Lady Soothcoor and Dr. Lakewood, "though I should like to have a quick word with Lady Amblethorpe before the concert."

James looked around. "Yes, you are correct, my love.

Excuse us, Lady Soothcoor, Dr Lakewood," James said, with a slight inclination of his head before he led Cecilia away.

"Lady Amblethorpe, Janine!" Cecilia enthused as they approached Lady Amblethorpe and her daughter Janine near the doorway.

Cecilia and Janine exchanged cheek kisses. They had become friends when Cecilia was investigating her husband's death. At one time she'd considered Lord Havelock, now Janine's fiancé, as one of the murderers. Janine had been quite vociferous in her defense of the man, even when all the evidence strongly suggested his guilt. It turned out Janine's instincts and loyalty were well-founded, for Lord Havelock had actually been a government agent investigating the disappearance of young women.

"What are you doing in town?" Janine asked.

"An emergency brought us here," Cecilia said.

"Oh?" Mrs. Amblethorpe asked, for that lady had a fondness for gossip.

"There was a kidnapping from the dock two days ago," Cecilia said softly.

"Oh, no!" Janine said. She reached out her gloved hand to Cecilia. She understood how such an event could affect Cecilia.

"Not the same as last spring, I am relieved to say," Cecilia hurried to add. "But related to this, I'd like to ask if there will be a break in Mrs. Billington's program to allow her to rest a few minutes and have refreshments?" Cecilia asked.

"Oh yes," Lady Amblethorpe said. "She quite insisted on it."

"Good. During that break I would ask a boon of you," Cecilia said.

"And what is that, my dear?"

"I should like to make an announcement to the assembled guests and a bit of a request."

"A request?" echoed Janine.

"Yes, you see a child has been forced into an apprenticeship with a chimney sweep. He never should have been in a position for this to happen."

"I don't understand," said Lady Amblethorpe.

"The Earl of Soothcoor's nephew, Christopher Sedgewick, the Honorable Owen Sedgewick's son, arrived in England two days ago and was kidnapped off the dock as he and his nursemaid were attempting to arrange transportation to the Soothcoor London home."

"What?" Lady Amblethorpe and Janine said. They looked at James for confirmation. He nodded.

"It is true," he said solemnly.

"There is a Bow Street agent on the case; however, my idea," Cecilia said eagerly, "is to have everyone in society request their chimneys be swept—it is that time of year, after all—and to have their staff, who will have the direct communication with the sweep, to be on the lookout for the little boy."

"But how should they recognize him? All sweeps have small climbing boys." said Lady Amblethorpe.

"He has the same downward slanted eyes Soothcoor and his brothers have, though his are brown. The set of the eyes carries strongly in the male line."

"They are quite distinctive," Janine agreed. "And you say the child has them?"

"Yes. We have seen a portrait of the child. It is quite amazing the strong resemblance to Soothcoor. Bow Street has had flyers made up with an etching of the boy's face that they are passing out. We have them as well, and our staff is distributing them to their peers. I think it would be wonderful if society would encourage their staff. There is a five-hundred-pound reward for the recovery of the child."

The ladies' eyes opened wide at the reward amount. "I should like to see this flyer," Janine said.

"I have one in my reticule," Cecilia said enthusiastically, as she opened the reticule and pulled out the flyer. She showed it to Janine and her mother.

"There is a strong family resemblance," Lady Amblethorpe admitted. "But announcing it at my musicale?" her voice announced her doubt.

"Mother, it is not like Lady Branstoke wants any of your guests to search for the child. It is something their staff can do," Janine said.

"But it is such a depressing subject for an uplifting night," she complained. "I want people to enjoy themselves. How can they enjoy themselves thinking of kidnappings? No, no, no. I can't allow it," Lady Amblethorpe said.

"Mother!" Janine stomped her foot. "This is not the time of year for selfish behavior."

"Selfish? How can you say that, Janine, when I wish others to have fun!"

"Yes, at the expense of a child." She looked at Cecilia. "How old is the child?"

"He's five."

"Five. So young," exclaimed Janine.

"He was sent to England by his father, because Owen Sedgewick's doctor in India told him he had not long to live."

"What of his mother?" asked Lady Amblethorpe.

"She died over a year ago."

Lady Amblethorpe pursed her lips as she looked down.

"Mother?" said Janine softly.

"For Lord Soothcoor," James said. "The child is Soothcoor's heir. Our friend would want us to find his heir."

"Lord Soothcoor is an honorable gentleman—if

perhaps lamentably a trifle dour at times," admitted Lady Amblethorpe.

James smiled and exchanged glances with Cecilia. "He is, at that."

"All right. You shall make your announcement when Mrs. Billington takes her break. I only ask you don't harm the mood of the evening."

"We shall earnestly try to remain positive."

Lady Amblethorpe nodded, then drew herself up. "Now, where can Mrs. Billington be? She went to freshen up before she begins and to get something to drink. She said she hadn't realized how much greeting everyone would have dried out her throat. I do hope she has not affected her voice. I should be ever so depressed if I caused her distress."

Cecilia recognized the change of subject as the end of the Soothcoor discussion. "I'm sure a moment or two of quiet will revive her."

"I keep remembering now that it was ill health that led her to retire from the subscription Vocal Concerts," Lady Amblethorpe said.

"Yes—however, she appears quite recovered and eager to sing again for an audience, Mother." said Janine.

"I believe that is she approaching now," said James, looking past Lady Amblethorpe. "Cecilia, we had best find seats."

"Yes. I'd like to sit close to the front."

"Excuse us Lady Amblethorpe, Miss Amblethorpe," James said, nodding to each woman. He led Cecilia toward the rows of chairs.

~

JAMES STOOD and extended his hand to his wife. "Come, before others rise for refreshments," he whispered, as

Mrs. Billington informed the audience there would be a short intermission.

As they approached the front of the room, the noise around them rose as guests talked amongst each other.

"James, I don't think I should be heard in this crowd," Cecilia lamented, as she looked about the room.

Her husband patted her arm. "I will get their attention."

They stopped in front of the musicians' discarded instruments. Suddenly, a sharp, shrill whistle blared across the room. All voices stopped and eyes turned toward the source of the noise.

James smiled. "Forgive me my rude whistle," he said.

"Bloody childish, wouldn't have thought that of you, sir," complained a man to their right.

James glanced in his direction. "Yes, desperate times require desperate measures."

"What is going on?" asked a woman in front of them. The voices around began building again.

James held up his arms. "Please, I just require a moment of your time."

"Two days ago, a five-year-old child disembarked with his ayah from a ship that had sailed from India. He'd been sent to England to live with his uncle. While on the wharf, he was stolen away from his ayah, and Bow Street has learned he has been sold into apprenticeship to a chimney sweep."

"That is disturbing that this should happen, Sir James, but why have you disrupted our evening to tell us this? The wharf areas are full of crime. I'm surprised Bow Street would even get involved."

"The child is Christopher Sedgewick, the son of Owen Sedgewick."

"*Natural* son, Sir James," called out Lady Soothcoor from across the room.

"That remains to be determined and is immaterial," Cecilia said repressively, staring frostily at Lady Soothcoor.

The guests looked from one woman to another, detecting juicy gossip fodder in a hidden story here.

"In my household, my housekeeper arranges for our chimneys to be swept. In yours, it may be the housekeeper or another upper servant. My staff have shared a flyer with an etching of the boy with their peers in the city, encouraging chimney sweeps to be hired and their climbing boys reviewed. Support your staff if they wish to get your chimney swept. That is all we ask."

"Climbing boys are black with soot. Who can recognize one from another? Your intention is honorable, sir, however not practical," said a man with a chin-strap beard.

"How many of you have noted the unusual downward slanting of the Earl of Soothcoor's eyes?" James asked.

"Like a soulful puppy," one matron close to him murmured.

"Exactly, Lady Fortner, like a soulful puppy. This child has unmistakable eyes like his uncle, the Earl."

A woman in the center of the room gasped. "I think I might have seen him! Does he have brown eyes, not gray like his uncles? Remember, Iona, when I told you about the child that looked like a young Alastair?"

"I do," said the older woman standing next to her.

The guests began talking. They gathered closer.

"I have a flyer with his picture," Cecilia said. She negotiated her way through the crush of guests. They moved aside to let her pass, curiosity now high in the room. She dug through her reticule again to pull out the picture and thrust it into the woman's hands.

The woman opened the folded parchment. Tears sprang into her eyes and slid down her cheeks. She raised a shaking hand to her lips as she stared down at the picture. "Oh, no," she whispered.

"This is the child you saw?" Cecilia asked.

The woman compressed her lips tightly and nodded.

The noise of the crowd grew louder, as word of what the woman said spread through the room.

James came to Cecilia's side and placed his arm around her.

The woman sniffed, then laughed as she fumbled for her handkerchief. James handed her his.

"I've taken a house on Mount Street," the woman explained, her voice redolent of a gentle Scottish accent. "We haven't moved in and are currently staying with the Viscount and Viscountess Syford. I am still hiring staff. I was at the house conferring with my new butler when a chimney sweep and two climbing boys arrived to clean the chimneys," she said, her eyes not leaving the paper she held.

Around them the room was quiet, the guests pressing close to hear what the woman said.

"The older boy was instructing the younger one on how to climb the chimney. The younger boy didn't want to and was trying to get away. The older boy threatened to burn him with the torch if he didn't start climbing. I protested, but the older boy said this always happens with the new ones, and not to worry. I didn't know what to think, but at that moment Mr. Curlings, my new butler, told me a housekeeper candidate had arrived for an interview. I looked back at the climbing boys and the younger one that looked so like a young Alastair Sedgewick. The child was climbing the chimney, so I assumed what the older boy told me was true and I left the room."

"Do you know the chimney sweep's name?

"No, I do not, but my butler most likely will. The

older boy did call the younger one something like Tristan."

"Could he have said Krishan?" Cecilia asked.

"Yes, it could have been that."

"Is the butler already living at the house?"

"Yes."

"I'd like to send the Bow Street agent to talk to him."

"Of course! And my name is Montgomery. Lilias Montgomery. I am a widow, and I have brought my family to London so my daughter Aileen might have her come-out under her great aunt's auspices," she said, indicating Viscountess Syford.

"Might I call on you tomorrow?" Cecilia asked. "Oh, forgive me, I am Lady Cecilia Branstoke, and this is my husband, Sir James Branstoke."

"I should be happy to receive you," Mrs. Montgomery said softly. "Might I keep the flyer?" she asked.

"Yes, of course!"

"Cecilia, we should go now so I might find Mr. Martin before it gets too late," James said.

James and Cecilia bid their farewells and hurried toward the doorway.

Cecilia stopped briefly to hug Lady Amblethorpe, who jerked back, startled.

"Thank you, Lady Amblethorpe, for granting us permission to speak. Your actions may lead us to solve the mystery of the missing child."

"You're quite welcome," said the flustered woman to their retreating backs, as the Branstokes hurried down the stairs.

# CHAPTER ELEVEN

Cecilia stared up at the bed hangings. She swore she had every fold and pattern memorized such that they stayed in her mind when her eyes closed.

But they weren't closed now and hadn't been for some while, and all she could do was stare and think.

She couldn't tolerate waiting for something to happen. She'd spent too many years in idleness. During her marriage to George Waddley, each day passed like the previous day, time passing with nothing different from one to the next, save the weather. She seldom even knew the day of the week for the sameness of her existence.

With her first husband's death, she'd been reborn. She became alive to the seasons, alive to the sounds and happenings around her, alive to her own thoughts and feelings. James had done much to awaken her to life. He did not treat her as a possession, a puppet for whom he pulled the strings. James welcomed her as a thinking, acting-upon-life woman—though sometimes he'd shake his head at what he deemed her machinations.

She smiled in the dark. Like the day he'd calmly trusted her to free herself of the ropes Stephen bound her with when they'd been tied up in the Woodhaven

Manor basement and nearly burned alive. He was amazing, this husband of hers. Outwardly unflappable and bored with life, inwardly preternaturally canny and alive to everything that went on around him. His outward mask was far better than the one she'd donned as a fragile, sickly woman. And he wore his mask effortlessly.

She turned her head to look at him sleeping beside her, only to find his eyes open, staring at her.

"You are awake. I thought you yet slept."

"I fear I have slept as little as you have," he replied, his voice rough with nighttime disuse.

"Hmmm. Yes." She turned he head to look up at the bed hangings again. "I don't like not knowing if Mr. Martin received our message or not."

"Nor I."

She turned back to face him. "We should go to Mount Street."

A slow smile pulled at his lips. "I knew you would say that."

"Well, if you did, why are we still lying abed?" She sat up, tucking her legs underneath her. "What time do you think it is?"

"Too early for your maid or my valet to be stirring."

"Then we shall fill those roles for each other." She leaned over to give her husband a kiss, then pulled back quickly before he could pull her down beside him as she knew he was wont to do.

"I suppose as I've become adroit at taking your clothes off of you, I can assist you in putting them back on," he drawled.

Cecilia laughed, threw back the covers and got out of bed, picking up the tinderbox and striker from the table and lighting the candle there.

"Why do we not have oil lamps in here?" she asked.

"Because they smell," James answered.

"Ah yes, there is that; however, sometimes they would be easier than candles." She opened the door to her dressing room. The water in the pitcher on the white-and-gilt dresser was cold, but she nonetheless poured it into the basin and splashed her face. She gathered clothing from her armoire and took it back to the bedroom she shared with James.

In the summer, she had been surprised and intrigued to discover her husband slept in the nude. However, in winter, in deference to the nighttime chill in the house, he donned a nightshirt. As he rose from the bed and stretched, Cecilia thought the nightshirt didn't matter—even covered as he was from his neck to his calves, he sent her heart deliciously fluttering. She was a lucky woman.

They dressed quickly and descended to the ground floor. The only staff they came across was a bleary-eyed footman lighting oil lamps in the foyer. He nearly dropped the glass globe cover to the lamp he was intent on lighting.

"Sorry to startle you, Nate," said James. He put on his hat as Cecilia donned her gloves. "Please unlock the door. Lady Branstoke and I have an urgent errand to attend to."

"Yes, Sir James." The young man replaced the glass globe and hurried to the door. "Shall I inform Cook to hold back breakfast until you return?"

"Yes. And inform my valet and Lady Branstoke's maid as well."

"Yes, sir." He bowed, then turned the locks and opened the door.

James grabbed Cecilia's hand and led her down the steps. A bluish-gray fog had settled in the streets, a dense blanket save for the dirty yellow circles of light on the ground around the still-lit street lamps. Eerily quiet, the morning struggled to push back the night.

"Do you mind if we walk?" James asked. "It's not far, and I'm loath to take the time to summon a carriage—if we could obtain one this early."

"No! Not all. So long as you continue to hold my hand," she said, coyly smiling and stealing a glance up at him.

"Minx."

"Seriously, walking arm in arm is so staid and stodgy sometimes. And one must admit it is not conducive to rapid progress" she said, fairly running to keep pace. "James! It would behoove you to remember you have longer legs than I," she complained, her voice growing breathy.

"I beg your pardon, my love." He stopped and drew her closer to him as he looked about. "It has come to my attention that the only souls out this early in the morning are the chimney sweeps. I have seen two groups as we've been walking—neither with a small boy. It occurs to me this is the hour of chimney sweeps. They need to do their work on cold chimneys before the day's fires are laid."

He paused a moment, as Cecilia looked at him. "What is it?" he asked.

"How is it that you know about chimney sweeps and their habits?" she asked.

He thought seriously about her question, his head canted. "I'm not sure other than I read, I listen, and I observe," he said.

"And commit to memory that which most of us would forget once our eyes moved on."

His eyes narrowed. "I believe it is more about observation. See on that roof across the street? There is a sweep up there."

"Where? And how can you see in this fog?"

He smiled. "Look up. "Up there to the left. By the chimney pots. I think he is using one of those mechanical devices I've read about. Many people don't like them, they don't think they do as good a job as a climbing boy."

"Ah," she acknowledged. They began walking again. "You are always so observant," she said, with a touch of jealousy coloring her tone. He always saw things before she did. It was maddening.

He smiled softly. "Years of training," he said.

"Military training," Cecilia concluded.

He inclined his head. "As you say, military training."

She noted he didn't explain himself. He never did about that part of his life—at least not yet. She wasn't as observant a person as he was, but she was sensitive to what was left unsaid.

"The house Mrs. Montgomery has taken is the next house down," James said.

They climbed the steps. James pounded on the door as Mrs. Montgomery's knocker had not yet been installed.

A man who looked like a pugilist in butler attire opened the door, scowling. "The knocker's off. There is no one home," he fairly growled.

"Yes, Mrs. Montgomery informed us she hadn't moved in yet. We are actually here to see you," James said.

"Me?"

"You are Mr. Curling, Mrs. Montgomery's new butler, are you not?" James cajoled.

"Yes." The man's wariness made James smile.

"I am Sir James Branstoke, and this is my wife, Lady Branstoke. Might we come in? It's deuced hard trying to stand talking at the door."

The man frowned; however, he did pull the door open to allow them to enter.

"We understand from Mrs. Montgomery you had the chimneys cleaned yesterday."

The man looked at them askance, but nodded. "Didn't know when they were last cleaned so decided it was safer to get them cleaned before Mrs. Montgomery moved in."

"Excellent notion. What we would desire to know is the name, and direction if you know it, of the chimney sweep."

The butler shook his head. "Don't know his direction, but said his name was Peasey, Percival Peasey."

"Peasey. Excellent. With that we should be able to locate him. Thank you," James said, turning to leave."

"Oh, if you wants to find him now, he's across the street," he added.

"What?" Cecilia and James turned back to look at the butler.

More relaxed now, he went on. "Lady Newcombe's butler came by when the sweep was here with his climbing boys. Said he wanted to engage him for today."

"We saw a sweep on a roof across the street and down a bit as we approached. Would that be the house? The light-gray townhouse?" James asked.

"Yes, sir."

"One last question," Cecilia said, as she pulled another flyer from her reticule. "Does this look like one of his climbing boys?"

The butler took the paper from her and pulled it close to his eyes. He squinted as he peered down at it.

Cecilia and James exchanged glances. The man needed glasses. Cecilia doubted he could discern the features of the child. She wondered if Mrs. Montgomery was aware of her new butler's vision challenge.

"Can't say rightly," he said, "however, I think so. The little one."

"Thank you. We will leave you to your day. You

have been most helpful." James opened the door and escorted Cecilia through it.

"I thought you said the man was using a mechanical arm sweeper," Cecilia said, as James hustled her down the steps.

"It appeared so. He may use both. Let's find out."

"I wish we could get word to Mr. Martin."

"As do I, but if we leave to attempt to contact Mr. Martin, he may finish up here and be gone. We cannot chance that."

More people and conveyances were appearing on the street, as much for the later hour as well as the fog lifting. They had to wait for a tinker's cart to pass before they could cross the street.

James rapped the door knocker. A footman opened the door. "Lady Newcombe is not available," he said. "You shall have to come back later." He started to close the door; however, James's booted foot stopped him.

"We've come to speak to the chimney sweep," James said, keeping his voice neutral.

"The chimney sweep?" repeated the footman, confused.

"Yes. We believe he is here with two climbing boys?"

The footman unconsciously relaxed, and he stepped back. "Yes, he's on the roof."

James used the moment to push the door open and pull Cecilia inside with him.

"And the climbing boys?" Cecilia asked.

"In the parlor, madam," the footman said, pointing vaguely to one of the closed doors on the left.

"Take me to the chimney sweep," said James.

"I can't! Mr. Konrude… Let me get Mr. Konrude," said the flustered footman.

"Quickly, then," Cecilia said.

"Sir James? Is that you?" came a thin, reedy voice from the stairs.

"Lady Newcombe!" warmth and delight colored James' voice. He quickly strode toward the staircase to meet the elderly woman, elegantly attired in a plum-colored morning gown coming down the stairs. He took both her hands in his and kissed her knuckles. "It is a delight to see you! I am actually surprised to see you in the city still."

"I don't leave for Newcombe Hall until St. Nicholas Day. I love my grandchildren; however, they fatigue me, and I keep my Christmas visit to strictly between St. Nicholas Day and Twelfth Day. That is long enough! It will take me two months to recover," she confided.

James laughed. "Let me introduce you to my wife." He led the elderly woman tenderly across the foyer.

"Lady Newcombe, may I present Lady Cecilia Branstoke. Cecilia, this is Lady Newcombe. She is a great friend of my mother's, and our two families often visited as I was growing up."

"I have fond memories of those years," Lady Newcombe said nostalgically. Then briskly, looking over her wireframed glasses at James, "But what brings you and your beautiful bride to my home, I'm sure it wasn't to visit an old woman."

He acknowledged her observation with a nod. "You have a chimney sweep here today," he stated.

"Yes," she said slowly.

"We need to speak to him and see his climbing boys."

She drew her head back, her brow furrowing. "Whyever for?"

"If the chimney sweep is the fellow who did the chimneys across the way yesterday, one of his climbing boys may be a child we are looking for."

"A child you are looking for? What do you mean?" She shook her head, obviously confused.

"A small boy was kidnapped from the East India

Docks three days ago," Cecilia said softly. "They afterward sold him into service to a chimney sweep. We have reason to believe he is now apprenticed to the chimney sweep cleaning your chimneys."

"I am confused. Why do you have an interest in this child? I'll grant you a child kidnapping is disturbing, but the child sold into service to a chimney sweep, or a blacksmith or a tailor or other trade is not unusual. It is often to the benefit of the child."

James inclined his head. "I understand. I am not in favor of the practice; however, I understand the practice." He patted her hand and sighed deeply. "In this circumstance, the child is not from the poorer denizens of our city. He is the nephew of the Earl of Soothcoor."

Lady Newcombe's face drained of color. "A member of society? Who is his father?"

"Owen Sedgewick. He had sent his son, Christopher, to England with his nursemaid. Sedgewick was in fragile health and wanted his son to be with family in case anything happened to him."

"I say, what's going on here? I'll take care of things, my lady," said a granite-faced gentleman without a whit of hair on his head. He strode toward them from the back hallway, the footman scurrying behind him. The man's lip curled at James and Cecilia as he rudely looked them up and down.

"It's quite all right, Mr. Konrude," Lady Newcombe loftily assured her butler as he approached.

"But—" the butler began, coming to stand near her.

"Forgive Mr. Konrude," Lady Newcombe said as she extended her arm gracefully to stop him coming closer. "He hasn't been with me long. My butler retired last month, and my son's steward hired Mr. Konrude for me."

Cecilia raised an eyebrow at the man's manner and expression, and more so at the set-down Lady Newcombe gave him with her tone and countenance. She exchanged glances with James, a half-smile pulling at her lips.

"It is quite all right, Lady Newcombe. It is an early hour for callers. As I said, we would like to speak with the chimney sweep and his climbing boys, if we may," said James. "I saw the sweep on your roof, and according to your footman, the boys are in the parlor."

Mr. Konrude frowned. "Tom, go up to the roof and ask Mr. Peasey to come down here, please."

"I will go with Tom to speak to him," James said. "It will be quicker that way."

The butler glowered. "Hmph. All right. Tom—"

"Yes, sir." Tom hurried forward. "This way, please, sir."

"And I should like to see the climbing boys," said Cecilia, speaking to Lady Newcombe. She undid the buttons of her pelisse and shrugged out of it. She held it out to the butler. He automatically accepted it. She undid the ribbons of her bonnet and handed that over, as well as her gloves.

"I have a picture of the child we are looking for," she told Lady Newcombe, once the butler had taken her outer wear. "He looks startlingly like his uncle."

"What is this?" Mr. Konrude demanded.

"Nothing to concern you, Mr. Konrude," Lady Newcombe said repressively. "I'll accompany Lady Branstoke to the parlor. See to Lady Branstoke's garments, then have tea brought to the parlor and some refreshments for the boys."

"Climbing boys? You're going to give refreshments to *climbing boys*?"

"Mr. Konrude, if you would stay in my employ, do not question me, no matter what instructions my son's steward may have given you to the contrary."

"Begging your pardon, my lady," he said sullenly, his frown close to a pout.

"And do learn to smile," she added, as she walked with Cecilia toward the parlor.

~

THE ACCESS to the roof was through an attic dormer window between two servant rooms. The window was open. James leaned out the window. There was a narrow ledge. The mansard-style slate roof went up almost vertically, then bent again at a shallower pitch. He could see where the chimney sweep had used a rope and hook to grapple a chimney and pull himself up the steep, slippery part of the slate roof.

He carefully stepped out on to the ledge. He could hear whistling from above him. At least the sweep was happy in his work.

He used the rope to pull himself up, then the ledger stones set like steps along the edge of the house wall forming the chimney, to walk up the shallower pitched roof. The chimney sweep had his back to him, pulling his mechanical device out of one chimney pot.

"Mr. Peasey," James said.

The chimney sweep twirled around. Seeing James, he swung the mechanical device at him.

James dodged the piece of equipment. "Stop! I want to talk to you!"

Mr. Peasey ran along the roofline to the chimney on the other side of the house, down the steps, then slid down the steep portion of the roof to the narrow ledge. James came down the side he'd come up, sliding down the rope to the ledge only moments after Mr. Peasey.

Peasey made a dash for the open window.

James grabbed the man's vest as he dove through,

pulling James after him. They landed together on the hall floor. "Peasey!" James grunted.

The man fought to get away, and they crashed against the walls as James tried to maintain his grip. The chimney sweep was wiry and strong; however, James had the advantage of height and weight. He got his arm around the chimney sweep's neck in a choke-hold. "Damn you! Stop it! Stop it!"

The sweep stilled, but James could tell by the tensed muscles he was only waiting for a chance to escape.

"I want to talk to you about your new apprentice."

He felt some of the tenseness release in the sweep. He loosened his hold a little so that Peasey could talk.

"Who offered the child to you as an apprentice?"

The sweep shook his head. James tightened his hold again. "I was in the peninsular wars," he said in the sweep's ear. "I know ways to hurt you," James said menacingly.

The sweep's eyes opened wide, and he suddenly relaxed, the fight gone. Slowly, James released him. "We want the man who sold the boy to you in apprenticeship."

"Why?" the sweep croaked.

"Because the child is the nephew of a peer of the realm."

The chimney sweep shook his head. "Nah, he ain't. You got da wrong chile and da wrong sweep."

"I don't think so. Dark hair darker complexion, and dark eyes that droop like a puppy dog's eyes."

"Yah."

"Answers to Krishan."

The sweep shook his head violently. "Nah, that's Tristan."

James laughed mirthlessly. "No, you mis-heard. It's Krishan, or Christopher Sedgewick."

"I didn't know," the man whined. "I needed a boy that size. He's perfect fer climbing chimneys."

"I will reimburse you for the cost of the boy, but you are going to help us find the man who sold him to you," James said as he released the man and rose to his feet.

The sweep slowly got up as well.

"Let's go," James said, leading him to the stairs.

"I didn't know," the man whined again.

James prodded him to go down the stairs.

# CHAPTER TWELVE

ady Newcombe's parlor was an elegant, Georgian-style room done in shades of pink with white and gold accents. They'd covered most of the furniture with Holland covers to protect the fabric from soot swirling in the air. The carpet had been rolled up and set in the back of the room. Canvas clothes covered the floor. At the fireplace Cecilia saw a dirty, older boy. He was looking up the flue.

"Git on wit'chya," he yelled up the chimney, his voice cracking between child and man.

An indistinct voice replied.

"Ya don't need ta see. Push yer broom ahead a ya and foller it up."

Scraping and scuffing sounds preceded chunks of soot raining down and scattering outward from the fireplace hearth.

The boy looking up, squeezed his eyes shut and pulled his head out from the chimney. He laughed as he shook the loose soot off himself. He was so covered in soot, there was no way to know his hair color. Light brown eyes shone out from his blackened countenance.

"Right, oh!" he exclaimed. "We'll make a sweep o' ya yet. Climb higher!"

"Gracious," Lady Newcombe said, as she looked the boy up and down.

Cecilia nodded wryly. She again removed the flyer from her reticule. She walked toward the climbing boy. "You, young man, what is your name?"

"Billy, ma'am."

"Billy, does this look like the child you have climbing up the chimney?" She held out the paper to the boy.

He tentatively took the paper from her, then looked down at it. "Coo! 'Tis the spittin'!"

"He should not be up that chimney. Tell him to come down immediately."

"But—"

"Immediately!—Oh, never mind," she said when he stood there staring at the paper in his hand. She walked past him to the fireplace and braced herself with one hand on the ornately carved surround below the mantle as she leaned forward.

"Christopher?" she called up. "Christopher Sedgewick?"

"Yes!" she heard a child's excited cry, followed by a yelp of pain. Soot rained down, catching her hair before she could pull away. She absently brushed away the bits in her hair, streaking her hand gray.

Up in the chimney, the child cried.

"Lady Branstoke!" cried Lady Newcombe. "You are getting soot all over yourself. Come away from there."

Cecilia shook her head. "Christopher," she said gently, leaning forward again. "You are going to be all right, Christopher. Can you come down now? You don't need to clean the chimney."

"Pro—promise?" she heard between sobs. Her heart clutched in her chest and her eyes began to tear.

"Yes, Christopher," she said, fighting her own tears, "I promise. Just come down."

She heard scraping and scuffing with more soot falling down. She bit her lower lip and clenched her skirts in her hands.

"Careful!" Billy warned, ducking his head into the chimney. "Slow, like I tol' ya."

Suddenly there was the sound of a harsh scrape against brick amid a flurry of dislodged soot falling.

"Ah-ah! Help! I can't move!" Wailing started again. "Help! Ouch, that hurts. I can't move!"

Billy ducked back into the fireplace. "What did you do?" he called up.

"I—I slipped! My legs, they're caught!"

The boy came out of the fireplace. "We need another climbing boy to climb up to him and pull on his foot."

Cecilia frowned. "Won't that hurt him more?"

The boy agreed. "Tear up his knees something awful."

"Can't you do it?" she asked.

He shook his head. "Me shoulders have grown too big."

Cecilia looked at the boy. He was her height, but he had broad shoulders. She didn't. She wondered if she could do it. "How do you climb up a chimney?"

"What?"

"Just tell me how to climb a chimney," she said fiercely.

"Well, ya get boosted up, and ya put yer back to one side, hard, then walk yer feet up till ya can't go more, then use yer hands to brace ya and lift yer arse higher, then walk yer feet ups agin."

She compressed her lips together, her brows pulling together. "I'm going to try it. Can you give me a boost?"

"But yer's a lady! And yer be wearin' skirts."

"Lady Branstoke!" protested Lady Newcombe.

There was a commotion in the hall, and then Lewis and Daniel Wrightson ran into the parlor.

"Pardon, Lady Branstoke," Lewis said, his sides heaving as he worked to catch his breath. "I didn't get your message until this morning. The butler at Mrs. Montgomery's said you'd come here."

"And he's here!" Cecilia cried, running over to Lewis. She lightly touched both his and Daniel's forearms. "Oh, Mr. Martin, he's here. But he's stuck in the chimney." She turned to Lady Newcombe. "I beg your pardon, Lady Newcombe. This is Mr. Martin—he is a Bow Street agent."

Lewis crossed to the fireplace and stooped to look up like Cecilia had. "Young Sedgewick, sir. Courage! We will get you out."

That brought more tears. Tears also streamed down Cecilia's cheeks.

"I was going to climb up to him. I'm small enough."

"I don't think that would be a good idea. You are not trained and could become stuck like Krishan," he said, using Miss Rangaswamy's pet name for him. He turned to the other climbing boy. "Do you know how far up he is?"

Billy pointed to the crown molding at the ceiling. "Nigh ter the next floor. Don't know how far he slipped, though," he said.

"Have you heard or seen of this happening before?" he asked, his sharp blue eyes studying the boy intently.

"Yes, sir." Billy looked down at his feet. "Most times they die."

Lewis shook his head. "That will not happen now," he said grimly.

"I didn't do nothing wrong!" exclaimed a rough voice, followed by a clattering on the stairs.

"If you didn't do nothing wrong, why did you take a

swing at me with your device and try to run?" It was James, his voice hard.

"Bloody hell, you're gentry. What's a poor chimney sweep to do?"

"Watch your language in a lady's house."

Krishan screamed.

Cecilia went back into the fireplace and stood up, her head in the flue. "We are here, Krishan," she called up, copying Lewis's mode of address to the boy. "We haven't abandoned you. We are trying to figure out the best way to get you out of there."

"It hurts! Don't leave me!"

"I won't. I'll stay right here. Can you tell me what hurts?"

"My head, neck and my back. My legs, too."

Cecilia inhaled sharply. He could break his neck with the strain if they didn't get him out of there soon.

"Cecilia, come out of there!" cried James, coming up to the fireplace.

"No, James," she said as calmly as she could for the child's benefit. "Christopher is scared. He needs me here. No, he really needs Miss Rangaswamy. Can you fetch her here?"

"Rani!" Krishan screamed on hearing her name. A new rain of soot showed Christopher had moved in the chimney.

Behind her, Cecilia heard Lewis's request to Dan Wrightson to fetch Miss Rangaswamy.

"Yes, Krishan. We are fetching her for you. You must be a good boy to wait, and please do not move. We will get you. I'll be here with you."

"Rani!" Krishan began crying again.

"It's okay, Krishan. You must be strong. You must be strong for Rani," Cecilia said as soothingly as she could, her own emotions and frustrations held in tight check, though she felt tears welling in her eyes. She felt as frightened as the child, and so helpless.

The flue was a tight fit, but she had some room to turn, but she scraped all around on rough ridges of excess mortar. She raised her arms and worked one and then the other above her head. She felt the surface of the brick. As the mortar was not neat and smooth as it would be on an outside surface, she could understand how a climbing boy worked his way up the walls and how slipping might cause painful and dangerous scrapes.

"James," she called to her husband, "Can you remove my shoes then lift me up so I can get closer to Krishan?"

"What are you planning, Cecilia?" he asked as he lifted her foot to remove one shoe and then the other.

"I'm small enough. I thought I could work my way up the flue like a climbing boy does."

"My love, your skirts would prevent you."

"I don't think so. They would just get ripped. I want to try, but I fear I have not the strength. That is what will prevent me. I would like to get as close to him as I can. Have you gentleman devised a plan?"

"I think so. Mr. Peasey is cooperating and is telling Mr. Martin we need to break though the wall right below where the boy is stuck."

"Break through the wall!" Cecilia exclaimed.

"Yes. Lady Newcombe has sent her footman to find ladders, chisels, and hammers, and anything else we might need. Mr. Martin and a maid are removing items from the mantel. Mr. Peasey said we need to come under him and reach in that way to support him, then work on removing more of the bricks upward until we can remove them where his legs are bent double. Then we can pull him out. Mr. Martin and I will do the work. We don't trust anyone else with Christopher's safety.

Now, I'm going to pick you up at your knees. Be ready. —Wait, Lady Newcombe has suggested a table be brought over for you to stand on, and Mr. Martin is doing that."

"Excellent idea! If I can't climb, a table will get me closer," she said.

"When I lift you, bend your knees so we can get the table here." He grabbed her and lifted her. Cecilia braced her arms against the sides of the walls of the flue and bent her legs. She heard the table move. The rough mortar bit into her flesh. She worried Christopher could have severe injuries.

James lowered her feet to the table and Cecilia pushed herself to stand up higher. She still couldn't reach Krishan, but she felt closer to him.

"Cecilia," James said, "the footman has secured one ladder and chisel and has left to procure another. Mr. Martin will start chiseling the wall. Those will be the sounds you and Christopher hear."

"Thank you," she said.

She tilted her head up toward Christopher. She couldn't see him but felt he might hear her better. "Krishan?" she said.

"Y-yes?" came his wavering voice.

"You are being very brave. Miss Rangaswamy will be proud of you. You are braver than me. I dislike how dark it is in here." The total darkness reminded Cecilia too much of the events from last May.

"I miss her," he said, sniffing.

"I know you do. But don't cry. She is coming. And we will get you out."

"But how?" he asked, his voice trembling.

"My husband says they will break through the wall underneath you."

"But how?" he demanded again, in the way only a young child would demand answers. Cecilia had to smile. If he could ask a child's "*how?*" question, he was bearing up well.

"I don't know, dear heart. I'm up here in the dark with you, so I can't see what they have planned."

In the flue, Cecilia heard noises coming from the wall, muffled pounding and ripping.

"Hear that, Krishan?" Cecilia asked. She felt she needed to keep the child talking, as much for him as for her.

"Yes. What is that?"

"They are opening up the wall. That is what that pounding you hear is. Once they get through the wall, they'll open up the chimney to get to you."

"All right."

"*Krishan!*" It was Miss Rangaswamy's voice.

"Rani! Rani" Krishan cried out excitedly, then howled in pain and soot poured down on Cecilia. She clamped her eyes and mouth shut tight.

"Krishan," Cecilia said sharply when the soot storm stopped, her heart in her throat that he should hurt himself more. She took a breath to speak softer. "Yes, she's here, but you must stay calm."

"What is it? What's wrong with my Krishan?" Miss Rangaswamy anxiously called up the flue.

"He's in a dangerous position. It is best if he not move," Cecilia called down to her, trying to not worry either Krishan or his ayah.

She heard James' muffled voice and Miss Rangaswamy's "Yes, yes," response. Then: "Cecilia?"

"Yes, James?"

"We are ready to start work on breaking through the chimney bricks."

"Excellent!"

"Yes, but before we do, I need you to come down out of the chimney. When we break through, bricks will fall on your head."

"Oh, I wouldn't like that," Cecilia said.

"No, I shouldn't either," he said.

"Krishan, my husband says they are going to break through the chimney, so I have to get down."

"I'm scared."

"I know you are, dear heart. But they are working as fast as they can to get you. Be brave for Miss Rangaswamy."

He sniffed. "Okay."

"James, you are going to have to help me," she called down to her husband.

"I will grab you as I did before. Daniel and Billy will pull the table away, then I can set you down."

"That would be perfect."

Once out of the fireplace flue, Cecilia blinked against the bright light and steadied herself as James returned to working on the wall. A long scrape on her forearm stung. She saw how filthy black her arms were, as was her ruined gown. No doubt her face and hair fared worse. She looked across the room. The parlor looked inordinately crowded. Mr. Thornbridge was in attendance, helping the gentlemen with the wall, and Mrs. Montgomery and Lady Syford were seated on the far side of the room, talking quietly to Lady Newcombe, each with a cup of tea in her hands.

Miss Rangaswamy ran up to her and grabbed her hand. "My Krishan, how is my Krishan?"

"I feel he is doing better than most children his age would. He is in pain, but he is trying to be brave for you, Miss Rangaswamy."

"Pain? How is he in pain?" Her cheeks wet with tears, she pulled against Cecilia to look up in the chimney.

Cecilia pulled her away. "It's not safe!"

"I don't care!" Rani exclaimed, struggling against Cecilia's hold.

"They are knocking a hole in the chimney now. Bricks will hit you. Who will care for Krishan if you are hurt? Listen to me. His neck and back are in an awkward position," Cecilia explained gently. "He is wedged in the flue with his legs drawn up to his chest, his back curved and his neck bent. I worry about his neck. We should have a doctor see to him right away before he is moved too much."

"But I must do!" Rani wailed.

"Help Daniel and Billy pick up the debris. It is dangerous for all of us to have the bricks and plaster and wood underfoot."

Lady Newcombe came up beside Cecilia. "I have sent for my physician, Lady Branstoke. He should be here, soon."

"Thank you for thinking of that."

She laughed gently. "It wasn't me, my dear, it was your devilishly smart husband who made the suggestion."

Cecilia laughed a little. "He is a bit prescient at times, to an extent that can be unnerving. Thank you, anyway, for following through with your own physician."

"Yes!"

Cecilia heard Lewis yell triumphantly from the ladder he stood on.

She looked up. The men had a hole about two feet in diameter in Lady Newcombe's wall above the fireplace. Cecilia bit her lip as she took in the devastation wreaked upon Lady Newcombe's beautiful parlor.

"Lady Newcombe, I am so sorry. We are destroying your parlor. I will have everything fixed afterward, I promise you."

"Piffle," Lady Newcombe said, dismissing the mess and the damage. "This is the most excitement I have had in years. And I shall dine out on this story for years to come!"

"I can see him," Lewis said, peering up into the hole they'd created. "We are about three feet too low; however, we can get to him."

"We need to secure a plank across, so he doesn't fall down the chimney as we work," James said, from the second ladder set against the wall next to Lewis.

"I got it, guv'nor," Mr. Peasey said. He handed the canvas rubbish bag he'd been holding to Mr. Thornbridge. "I'll nip out to da mews to fetch a plank. I knows what to look for."

Lewis looked at Daniel and jerked his head toward the door, silently instructing Daniel to follow him.

"Do you think he'll use the opportunity to run?" James asked.

"I wouldn't be surprised," Lewis said tiredly. He ran his hand through his hair. "I have questions for him, and he knows it. That's why I sent Daniel to follow him."

James nodded. He turned back to look at their progress on the wall. "I suggest we work at making the hole larger—without going upward yet, but enough to get our arms and shoulders in the chimney."

Lewis nodded. "We can pound spikes in the opposite wall and rest a board across the spikes and the opening here, to give us a bit of a platform."

They heard an ominous scrap from the chimney. Christopher slipped.

"We don't have time for niceties," James said grimly.

Lewis and James worked swiftly to pull more plaster and wood slats from the chimney flue to reveal more bricks.

"Are you all right, Master Sedgewick?" James asked.

"Yes," said the small voice. "Please hurry. My neck hurts. Is Rani still here?"

"Yes, she is standing below me, looking up and wringing her hands."

That drew a slight giggle from the child.

"Good lad," James said. He looked down. "Billy, see if you can find us some additional spikes. We will have to use the two we have to drive into the chimney, and we will need replacements to chisel out more bricks."

"Yes, sar," the older climbing boy said. Rani took the canvas rubbish bag from him. He ran out of the room.

"I'm sorry, Mr. Thornbridge. We have taken your rubbish runners away," said Lewis.

David shrugged with a grin. "With Miss Rangaswamy assisting in the collection, I can carry a canvas bag outside to be dumped."

"And I'll assist to take whatever you gentlemen pass down from your expansion work to fill another canvas bag," Cecilia declared.

James glanced down at her. Soot covered her, but her dark blue eyes shown out from her begrimed face. His love for her pressed upon him. For not the first time since he'd met her, he marveled at her tenacity. His wife was not one to shirk helping and didn't consider her size or sex as a hindrance. It seldom occurred to her she had a hindrance to even be considered! He'd never imagined he'd find a woman as inspiring as Cecilia.

"Miss Rangaswamy," Cecilia said softly, as they worked together, "we need to keep Christopher calm and still while James and Lewis work to get him out. He tells me his neck hurts. He is putting a great deal of strain on it. He needs to not move around or get excited, or I fear he could do himself permanent injury."

Cecilia watched Miss Rangaswamy's eyes widen. Fear glistened in her dark eyes. She licked her lips and nodded briskly.

"Yes, yes. I understand." She wiped at her eyes and

looked up at the hole Sir James and Mr. Martin had enlarged. "I am so proud of you, Krishan. You are calm and still like they ask. This is good!"

"Rani?"

"Yes, Krishan."

"I want to go home! I don't like this England place." He cried again.

Cecilia wanted to cry with him. Everyone glanced at one another. James and Lewis increased their efforts to chisel away the brick, wood, and plaster between them and Christopher.

"No, Krishan. We cannot go back for a while. Please don't cry!" She paused and looked around the room. "These are good people who are helping, you will see! I promise."

James angled his head into the hole in the wall. "Christopher," he said.

"Yes?"

"Mr. Martin is close to chipping away at the bricks pressing up against your legs. I am going to reach in now and take hold of your arm with one hand and support your back with the other. Do not move. It is important there are no sudden movements. Let us move you. Do you understand?" James kept his tone calm. The wrong move by himself or Lewis, and Christopher could fall down the chimney, or worse, snap his neck.

"Yes, sir," Christopher whispered. His voice strained.

James pushed his right arm and shoulder into the enlarged hole and stretched to reach under his back to support him. With his other arm he reached inside the chimney to take hold of Christopher's upper arm. He could feel Christopher's heart stampeding.

"Ready?" Lewis asked, poised to deliver another blow to the spike he'd been using as a chisel.

"We are ready," James said calmly, "aren't we, Christopher?"

"I'm scared."

James felt Christopher's body tense. He slipped another inch, his weight now heavy and ungainly across James' right arm. He inched himself farther into the hole.

"I have you. You won't fall," James assured him. James clenched his jaw. They were in a dangerous position.

"All right," Christopher said meekly, so forlorn.

"Let's get him out of here, Mr. Martin," James said.

Lewis hit the spike between the bricks a couple more times, then two bricks broke loose. He didn't even try to catch them as he had the others. Christopher's shin, free from the pressure on the brick, shot forward. Christopher screamed as he slipped, no longer wedged.

James' arm strained to hold him.

Lewis, a foot braced on the mantel, reached in and grabbed hold of Christopher's other arm and guided his feet to the opening. He helped James slowly draw Christopher out of the chimney.

"If you can, support his neck, gentlemen," said a new deep voice from below. "Lady Branstoke has told me of his position. There could be damage—let's keep it to a minimum."

James didn't recognize the man's voice, but at that moment he could have cheerfully throttled him. Now was not the time to be issuing orders. He felt his heart in his mouth as they gently pulled the child out.

Mutely, James and Lewis coordinated their efforts. Once they had Christopher out of the chimney, Lewis passed all of Christopher's weight to James.

The ladies having tea cried out and started clapping and laughing.

"Stay where you are. Don't try to come down the ladder yet," Lewis instructed James.

Lewis scrambled down his ladder, then pulled the table Cecilia and James had used over next to James's ladder. He jumped on top, then reached up to take the boy from James. Once he had him firmly in his arms, he crouched down to pass the child back to James after he descended the ladder. Miss Rangaswamy was before him, her arms outstretched.

Christopher saw her and jerked around. "Rani!" he cried, then screamed in pain.

Miss Rangaswamy wrapped her arms around him, cradling him against her. "You are safe. You are safe," she said, tears streaming down her checks.

Tears streamed down Cecilia's cheeks as she joined in the clapping. Christopher was safe.

# CHAPTER THIRTEEN

"*I*'d rather not give him laudanum right now, but he should stay still for at least the next twenty-four hours." Dr. Seeton rose from the chair he'd sat in next to Christopher's bed, to speak to Cecilia and Miss Rangaswamy. "He strikes me as an active child, so I fear that may be a tough request." He returned his instruments back to his bag as he talked.

"My concern is for his neck. Based upon my examination, I do not believe there is a gross injury; however, with the pain he claims, there could be significant soft tissue injury. He may have continued neck pain and stiffness for several days. And don't be surprised if the pain is worse with neck movement or, conversely, the neck becomes stiff, and he can't move it. He may suffer pain in his shoulders, back, or arms. Headaches can also occur that may start at the base of his skull. The only road to recover is complete rest and immobility."

Miss Rangaswamy nodded vigorously and sat down in the chair the doctor left.

"I understand," said Cecilia. She looked down at Christopher where he lay. He was now as clean as he could be without the benefit of placing him in a tub of hot water, which he sorely needed. Mrs. Dunstan and

Miss Rangaswamy had gently washed the worst of the soot from his body and rubbed his hair with a damp towel, then dressed him in a nightshirt Miss Rangaswamy had recovered from their trunks.

Based on Dr. Seeton's recommendation, they had used a plank as a stretcher to carry Christopher and transported him by carriage the few blocks to the Branstoke townhouse, while Lewis escorted Mr. Peasey to Bow Street for questioning. Young Daniel Wrightson and Billy volunteered to go ahead to the townhouse to alert the staff they were coming and—as Daniel told Billy on an aside—partake of food.

"Dr. Seeton, I hope you will stay and join us for a light luncheon. I'm certain my husband will want to discuss Christopher's condition. We expect the Earl of Soothcoor will be here in a day or two, and we will need to inform him of the details for Christopher's care."

"Thank you for the invitation; however, I must decline. I have other patients I need to check in on today."

"I understand. You certainly didn't have this morning's call on your schedule, and you have been good to spend so much time with Christopher."

"As a doctor, I am accustomed to my plans going astray. But you said you expect Lord Soothcoor to be here in a day or two? So soon? Didn't you say he was in Northumbria?"

"Yes, but knowing Lord Soothcoor's character, he will not make a leisurely journey back to London. Sir James predicts a multiple succession of horses will give out before Lord Soothcoor does," she confided wryly as they walked down the corridor from the nursery rooms to the stairs.

"I only met the man once, and he struck me as a dour individual."

She laughed. "He gives that appearance. I assure you, Dr. Seeton, that is all it is."

"Ah, self-protection?"

"I would say so. I don't know the particulars. Not yet. But I shall discover the truth, eventually."

Dr. Seeton laughed. "After seeing you in that chimney when I entered Lady Newcombe's parlor, I would wager you are a formidable woman when it comes to getting what you want."

"Oh, please, surely not *formidable*!"

"My lady, forgive my plain speaking; however, you do rise above the ordinary. I don't know another woman who would have climbed up into a chimney."

"He is correct, my dear," James said languidly from the landing. He looked at Dr. Seeton. "My wife never ceases to amaze me. She has the heart and soul of a tiger. And like that ferocious animal, she will go after her goal with no thought to her own safety, much to my fatigue."

"Fatigue!" protested Cecilia.

The hint of a smile answered her protest. "Come and eat. Dr. Seeton, will you join us?" James said.

"Sadly, no. I will be by to check on Christopher tomorrow, if that is all right."

James inclined his head. "I should expect no less. Come Cecilia, let the good doctor go, and come join Mr. Thornbridge and me."

They saw the doctor out, then walked together to the dining room.

"How is Christopher?" James asked.

"There are no broken bones. Dr. Seeton is concerned for a neck sprain, much as he might get if he was learning to ride and was thrown off his horse. He does not want him to move his head around at all for several days."

James nodded. "Yes, I have heard neck injuries can

plague a person for life if not given the opportunity to heal properly. And what about you? I saw a nasty looking scrape on your arm."

Cecilia self-consciously grabbed her forearm. "After I took my bath, Dr. Seeton bandaged it for me. It is but a scrape. He has applied several bandages to Christopher's scrapes as well. That mortar was sharp!"

James nodded as they approached the door to the dining room. A footman was before them to open it.

"Do you think we will hear from Mr. Martin today?" she asked.

"Yes, he said as much before he went off with Mr. Peasey. He believes Peasey knew there was something nefarious about the apprenticeship purchase, but if the man is as cagey as Martin thinks he is, he will deny it and play innocent, and he won't be able to arrest him. Instead, he will have him followed to see if he leads them to who sold the boy to him to get his money back. It is that person Mr. Martin wants to speak with. He feels it is too coincidental that the kidnappers happen to lock Christopher in a room, and it just so happens someone gets into that room and steals Christopher away."

"Hmm. I would have to agree."

"Mr. Thornbridge," Cecilia said, when they entered the dining room, "thank you for your help today. How did you happen to be here when Daniel came to get Miss Rangaswamy?"

"I came to inform you that the son of the prospective buyers of Waddley's Spice and Tea wants a tour of our warehouses this afternoon. Do you want to be there?"

Cecilia looked at James. He shrugged his shoulders slightly, his expression enigmatic. She turned back to Mr. Thornbridge, her lips compressing. She sighed. "Normally I would say 'yes.' However, today I prefer to allow you to handle the tour, Mr. Thornbridge. I do not need to be there. It would just be my insatiable need to control that would have me there."

Out of the corner of her eye, she saw James's smile. She turned to him. "What?"

"I shall tuck your admittance to a need to control in a safe corner of my mind. I might need to haul it out to remind you some day."

"Oh, you!" She flicked her serviette at him. "I'll allow I wrestled with being here for Christopher and keeping up with the sale of Waddley's. Christopher is far more important, and I know, Mr. Thornbridge, that you will appropriately represent Waddley's. Who is coming?"

"Damon Partridge."

"Demon Damon himself," James said with a laugh. "Best you are not there, Cecilia. Demon Damon has a certain reputation with the ladies."

"What, do you not trust me?"

"It is not you I don't trust," James said pointedly. "He is an excellent businessman, very shrewd—best be on your toes, Mr. Thornbridge."

"He will probably nose about to find any reason to lower the price or gain other concessions from me. Do not give him any," Cecilia cautioned. She lowered her hands to her lap as she thought for a moment. Then she picked up her fork again. "Two can play his game," she said, before she took another bite of her lunch.

David grinned. "Yes, my lady."

~

CECILIA WENT UP to the nursery after lunch and discovered Miss Rangaswamy gently massaging Christopher's neck and shoulders, while Mrs. Dunstan sat in the corner working on a sewing project.

"What are you doing?" she asked, alarmed.

"Ayurvedic massage," Rani said. "A healing massage. It is to get his energies flowing through his body. Right now, his muscles are congested. Blood needs to flow to help the healing."

Cecilia looked at Christopher. "How does it feel, Christopher?" she asked.

His face twisted into a puzzled grimace. "It hurts where she touches and then feels better."

"I am only doing a gentle touch. I have told Christopher he will need to lie still. He does not like that," she said, with a loving smile at Christopher.

"And we know how difficult it is for young boys to be still, so I am making a head-and-neck brace," said Mrs. Dunstan. She held up what looked like part of a corset.

Cecilia cocked her head to the side as she looked at it, then walked toward Mrs. Dunstan to get a closer look. "Is that a corset?"

Mrs. Dunstan laughed. "It was before we started alterations. We got the idea from those impossibly tall shirt collars and cravats that the Dandies wear. They can't turn their head. We need the same thing for Christopher."

"How clever! It does look like it will serve," Cecilia enthused. "Still, he probably won't like wearing it."

"No—however, if wearing it means he can get out of bed, I can see that as incentive."

"We realized he needed something like this if he was going to eat. It is hard to swallow lying flat on one's back. We have tried to feed him some lunch...it was difficult for him. Hopefully by dinner time I shall have this done, and we can let him sit up to eat."

"You ever amaze me, Mrs. Dunstan. First with the nursery rooms, then your unstinting help with Miss Rangaswamy, and now this. You are a gem. I am delighted to have you in our employ."

A deep pink blush suffused Mrs. Dunstan's cheek. "Thank you, my lady."

A knock on the open nursery door drew Cecilia's attention. She turned.

"Excuse me, madam, Sir James said to inform you that Mr. Martin has arrived," Charwood said from the doorway.

Cecilia noted the glare he cast Mrs. Dunstan and concluded he had heard her complimenting the woman. She didn't know what had happened to their butler. He had been the absolute perfect butler when she and James married. In the months since then, he seemed to have morphed into a person she did not know. She would need to discuss his behavior with James. Perhaps he could get to the root of the man's issues.

She took her leave of Christopher, Miss Rangaswamy, and Mrs. Dunstan and followed Charwood downstairs. The butler led her past the parlor to the library. James and Lewis sat at a card table near the windows and rose as she entered the room. On the table were the brandy decanter and their glasses. Strewn across the table were papers and the flyers with penciled notes in the margins. She took one look at their activities and turned to Charwood and requested tea be brought for her.

"It did not take you long with Mr. Peasey," Cecilia observed as she crossed the room and took a seat at the table.

"No, my lady," Lewis said, as he sat down opposite her. He ran his hand through his blond hair as he shook his head, his expression grim. Both he and James had removed their jackets and rolled up their shirtsleeves. "I didn't really expect it to. Two junior officers will follow him. We are hoping he will seek whoever sold Christopher to him as an apprentice."

"Didn't he question the shade of Christopher's skin? Wouldn't that have provided a hint that this was not a poor child?"

"He said he thought Christopher was Romany. He didn't question his good fortune to be offered the child, as his size was ideal and his understanding superior to most small children of his age."

"I should think so. Just hearing him speak should raise questions."

"One would think so. He claims his desperation for help overruled questions."

"I can't believe Christopher was eager and willing to be his apprentice, either. I would think he would object and try to tell him who he was."

"There are many holes in his story—however, nothing we can prove to press charges for. Buying apprentices is common practice, and the new apprentice does not need to be willing."

"Disgusting. James, we really need to bring this forward."

James nodded. "We'll discuss it with Soothcoor. He would be the one to advise us on whom to approach."

"I should like to talk with Christopher when his initial trauma has worn off and he is more comfortable. He may have overheard names or seen things that are important."

"I should prefer to wait until after Dr. Seeton has seen him again."

"I understand—however, consider. Someone wanted to separate Christopher from Soothcoor and was not afraid to make that a permanent separation. Luckily, so far, the hired resources have not been inclined to murder a child. We cannot take it for granted that all will be so loath."

Cecilia stared off across the room, her mind running in circles. She knew little about children, had not had the opportunity to learn anything of children. What was the correct action?

A shiver ran through her. "You think someone would go to murder?"

"They already have, else Muriel Patterson would still be alive."

~

CECILIA LED the way to the nursery and quietly pushed the door open. Rani yet sat by Christopher's bed. She'd been singing softly to him in her native language, but broke off when Cecilia, James, and Lewis entered.

"Is he awake?" Cecilia asked.

Rani looked down at him, then shook her head as she rose from her chair. She glanced at Mrs. Dunstan who waved her on to talk to Cecilia and Lewis.

"No," she said as she walked over to them. She looked back at Christopher again, then came out into the hall with them.

"I need to speak with him," Lewis said.

Rani glared at him. "He is but five, a child, a child in pain."

"I know, but even an innocent child hears things."

"No, you cannot wake him." She placed her hands on her hips, her posture stiff, and her brow pulled to-gether. The fierce protectiveness in Rani's eyes and manner caused Cecilia to smile.

"Mr. Martin, could you not tell Miss Rangaswamy the questions you would ask? She can ask them when he wakens, and he is more likely to truthfully tell her the answers to your questions than he would to you." Cecilia suggested.

He cocked his head. "Yes, that would be ap-propriate."

"Then let's go to my sitting room to discuss the

questions you have. That way, Miss Rangaswamy will not be far from Christopher, and that will help her relax as well."

"Thank you, my lady," Rani said, her face clearing. She sighed heavily.

Lewis smiled at her. "I do not mean to be a trouble, Miss Rangaswamy," he said gently. "I, like you, only want what is best for the child and believe fiercely we need to capture those involved in his kidnapping."

"I know," she said, almost shyly. She smiled slightly and looked down.

Cecilia, noting her reaction, raised her eyebrows and compressed her lips, but said nothing. It appeared Miss Rangaswamy was taken with Lewis. Interesting. And what a tangle if Mr. Thornbridge was truly enamored with her!

She led them to her sitting room.

Cecilia sat in the upholstered chair, which left her sofa for Lewis and Rani. "Mr. Martin, what would you have from Christopher?" she asked.

"Quite a bit I'm afraid," he admitted to her. He turned to face Rani. "I understand you may not be able to ask him all of my questions at once. And you may divine other questions that should be asked, based on his responses."

She nodded and pressed her clenched hands into her lap while staring at him intently. "Yes, yes," she said eagerly.

"I would like to know what he remembers the men said who took him from the woman. Did they mention any names? Did they say anything to him about their plans? When he was locked in the room above stairs at the tavern, how did that come about? What did they say or do then? Did he try the door to prove it was locked?"

"Oh! You think they left it unlocked for the next person to take him?"

"I honestly don't know what to think yet, Miss Rangaswamy, but I have to cover all contingencies."

"Yes, yes, I understand," she nodded vigorously. "And this is why you say to think of my own questions because of what he say?"

"Precisely," he said approvingly, angling more toward her on the sofa.

Cecilia wondered if she should stay in the room, so intently did the two of them look at each other. The reactions of each to the other quite took her interest. She felt like a voyeur but considered chaperone to be her role. An odd role for her!

"Ask him exactly how it happened that the other man came to get him out of the room and what that man said to him. Everything he can remember."

Rani shook her head. "You expect a great amount from a little boy."

He sighed, "Yes. And it might be he won't remember when you ask, but be alert if he says something of merit later."

"If we continue to tell him how brave he was, that may help toward alleviating any lingering anxiety he has and make him more comfortable with the memories. I wouldn't be surprised if the trauma didn't at first block some memories."

Lewis looked at her consideringly. "I hadn't thought of that, Lady Branstoke. I concede that might have an effect." He shook his head as he sighed. "I recognize my own impatience. My anxiety is someone may try to get to him again. I will ensure there are watchers on your property."

Rani reached out her hand and touched his forearm briefly. "You think they might, that my Krishan still be in danger?"

"I don't know, Miss Rangaswamy. However, I do know I am loath to take chances."

She nodded slowly. "Thank you for that," she said solemnly. "If that is all, I would get back to Krishan now. I will remember your questions."

She rose and Lewis did as well. "My lady," Rani said, as she curtseyed to Cecilia and went out the door.

Cecilia rose as she left. She looked at Lewis. "I shall prompt her should she forget, which may happen because of her anxiety over Krishan."

"Thank you, Lady Branstoke."

"And I shall tell Sir James about the watchers. He will not like it, but he will appreciate it, as do I."

# CHAPTER FOURTEEN

*A*fter staring up in the dark at the bed hangings she could only see in her memory and not falling asleep, Cecilia quietly got out of bed, drew on her dressing gown, picked up the candlestick, tinderbox, and striker from beside the bed, and carefully let herself out of the bedroom she shared with James. She lit the candle, slid the striker into the pocket she'd insisted be sewn in the dressing gown, and walked down the hall to the nursery. Their house was unusual for the nursery to be on the same floor as their bedroom and the guestrooms to be on the floor above. Cecilia surmised the previous owners had designed it that way, and she personally liked the plan.

It had humorously surprised her when Mrs. Dunstan had requested the use of the drapes from the dining room, when Cecilia had arranged for that room to be redecorated. She told Cecilia she wanted to brighten up the nursery *"Just in case,"* she'd said, with a smile and a wink.

Judging by the looks of the nursery in daylight, she had done more than add new drapes and clean the room. Some judicious use of paint had been done as well. She wondered how she had paid for that! In time, she would find out. She suspected some squeezing of the household budget. Cecilia determined to look at the household account books when all the excitement and mystery resolved.

She set the candle down on a table in the hall and turned to open the nursery door, only to see it opening. Mrs. Dunstan quietly backed out of the room and closed the door. Cecilia did not want to startle the woman, so she stepped away from the door.

When Mrs. Dunstan turned, she stepped back in surprise; however, she did not screech in alarm, merely raised a hand to her chest. She too was dressed in her dressing gown—a surprisingly bold red affair—and wore a nightcap on her head.

"Lady Branstoke! What are you doing up?" Mrs. Dunstan whispered.

"I couldn't sleep," she said. "So, I thought I would check on Christopher."

Mrs. Dunstan nodded. "I couldn't either—I thought I would relieve Miss Rangaswamy for a few hours."

"She wouldn't let you?" Cecilia asked, still on the barest breath of a whisper as they moved down the hall toward the stairs.

"Poor dear was lying on the floor by Master Christopher's bed, sound asleep. I went into her room, pulled the quilt off the bed, and laid it over her. I didn't have the heart to disturb her."

Cecilia squeezed Mrs. Dunstan's arm. "You did right, I think."

"I'm thinking of going to the kitchen for warm milk. Would you like some as well?"

"I think that is a splendid idea!" Cecilia said. "I need to relax and stop my mind from racing around. I keep thinking there are questions I should be asking that I'm not. Something Miss Rangaswamy has said, but I can't get them to coalesce in my mind, so my thoughts run in circles."

"Then yes, a nice cup of warm milk will be just the thing."

The women made their way silently down to the kitchen. Mrs. Dunstan busied herself with skimming the cream off the milk and pouring the milk into a pot on the stove. She stirred the embers and added more coal to get the fire going again. While she worked, Cecilia sat on a stool by the worktable.

"Have you talked to Miss Rangaswamy about her life in India?" Cecilia asked Mrs. Dunstan.

"A little, here and there," the housekeeper said as she stirred the milk. "She told me about Mr. Sedgewick's house and the medicinal plants growing around it."

"Medicinal plants?"

"Yes. Evidently Mrs. Sedgewick—if she *was* Mrs. Sedgewick—" Mrs. Dunstan began.

"I prefer to believe she was."

Mrs. Dunstan nodded, "As you say, madam. Anyway, she was a student of Ayurvedic medicine. She'd always been sickly with asthma, so she studied cures. It was one of her cures that helped Mr. Sedgewick, and he planted that vine all around the house, so excited to have a medicine that helped. Miss Rangaswamy said— rather wryly, I thought—at least the flowers were pretty."

"She didn't like the plant?"

"I don't know if she didn't like the plant or thought the number of plants was more than they could use." She poured the warm milk into cups and gave one to Cecilia. She sat on a nearby chair.

Cecilia nodded. They both cupped their hands around the warm cups and rested their elbows on the table.

"She is such a delightful little thing. She quite makes

me laugh when she stops thinking of her worries and just responds to life around her. She practically danced down the street the other day when we went to pass out more flyers. Everyone responded positively to her. Except for Mr. Charwood, of course," she finished, with a raised eyebrow and twisted lips.

Cecilia nodded and sipped her milk. "He has certainly changed, and not for the better. James said he will talk to him, but with everything going on, he hasn't had the opportunity to do so."

"I understand, madam, I do indeed."

Cecilia yawned broadly. "What else have you learned about Miss Rangaswamy?"

"She does not like to sew," Mrs. Dunstan said with a laugh. "Quite skewed up her nose when I suggested working for a modiste as what she could do for employment if Soothcoor would not take her on."

"I'm sure he will."

"Yes, such was my thought as well. But she doesn't want to make the mistake of complacency she made when her uncle told her his son would take care of her."

Cecilia pondered that determination for a moment as she took another sip of milk. She smiled as she looked across the table. "I admire her determination. Soothcoor will see that she's not left to fend for herself. That is not his way at all! However, she does not know that and is thinking ahead."

"I find myself quite proud of her, and why I should, I don't know, for I've only known her a few days. Nonetheless, I am," Mrs. Dunstan said. She set her cup down.

Cecilia yawned again and stretched. "She is an easy person to like. She is so sincere and natural, a trait I think many in London have lost." She stood up. "I think I can go back to sleep now. Thank you for your care and interest in Miss Rangaswamy. She needs support."

"She has it," Mrs. Dunstan said. "Good night, madam."

Cecilia made her way back upstairs to the bedroom and quietly slipped back into bed.

Not quietly enough, she realized, when James laid his arm over her and pulled her closer to him. She smiled in the dark and relaxed. As she slipped into sleep, she wondered what houses in India looked like.

OWING to her sleeplessness during the night, Cecilia woke late. She tossed on her dressing gown and went into her sitting room to ring for Sarah.

"Why did you let me sleep so long?" Cecilia exclaimed when Sarah entered some five minutes later, bringing with her a pitcher of hot water for the porcelain basin.

"Sir James said you couldn't sleep in the night and were wandering about. He said you needed your sleep today."

"Wandering about—hardly. I just went to check on Christopher. But Mrs. Dunstan was before me. She was kind enough to make me some warm milk to help me sleep.

"Ah then, that is why Mrs. Dunstan was later than normal below stairs," Sarah said with a half grin.

"That is enough!" Cecilia said, laughing. "And I'm afraid I shall require more than just that pitcher of hot water," she said, airily waving in that direction. "You did a good job of brushing the soot out of my hair yesterday, but I really need to wash my hair. I swear my scalp itches."

"I shall get with the footmen to bring up hot water. Should you also like a breakfast tray in here?"

"Yes, that would be lovely. "

Some minute later James came to her dressing room. "Cecilia, remember the investments Owen Sedgewick was involved in?"

"Yes?"

"Our solicitor's office has just sent over their findings regarding his investments. Remember the Paradise Medicinal investment mentioned?"

"Yes, I do. It was quite extensive."

"Guess who the partners are in that venture."

She shook her head. "I have no idea whom Mr. Sedgewick might be involved with."

"It listed one person as Alastair Sedgewick, Earl of Soothcoor."

"That makes sense."

"And the other is Damon Partridge."

"Damon Partridge of the Partridge and Sons Import and Export Company, who are buying Waddley's?"

"The same."

"Gracious." Cecilia blinked as she sat back on the sofa. "He visited Waddley's yesterday afternoon. Do you remember, Mr. Thornbridge asked if I wanted to attend?"

"I do. I think I shall visit Mr. Partridge," James said.

"James, I must wash the last of the soot out of my hair, and it will take a good two hours for my hair to dry. *Faugh!* I can't put it off, but there are so many other things I'd like to be doing. Like visiting Christopher!"

"And Dr. Seeton will be back this morning as well."

"I could not possibly visit Mr. Partridge today," she said.

"And perhaps that is a good thing."

"What do you mean?"

"I would speak to him of Paradise Medicinals, and I can do so without confusing the discussion with the upcoming Waddley Spice and Tea Company acquisition."

She thought for a moment. "I see what you mean. I will reluctantly agree with you, but you know how much I prefer to be involved."

He laughed. "I do indeed. I promise I shall make a full report to you on my return."

"Excellent. I must get my bath, now." She stood up. "Go." She waved him away.

He laughed again. It occurred to him he'd not laughed so much in his life until he'd married Cecilia. She was his delight. He left her to her new flurry of activity.

~

"CHRISTOPHER IS DOING WELL TODAY," Dr. Seeton said as he came out of the nursery an hour later. "He still has some muscle strain with pain, but not as much as I had expected."

"That is wonderful to hear. Please join me in the parlor, where we can discuss Christopher's condition and care," Cecilia said.

She had to rush to finish dressing when she heard Dr. Seeton had arrived. As it was, she couldn't speak to him until after his examination of Christopher. And perforce, with wet hair hanging down her back, she felt she looked the hoyden. Couldn't be helped.

She led him into her upstairs parlor. "Can I get you some tea? I need some. There is so much going on today with the worry about Christopher and the investigation I find a good cup of tea helps me to take a moment to relax and think."

"I should be delighted to share a pot of tea with you, Lady Branstoke," Dr. Seeton said.

She gave instructions to the footman, then invited Dr. Seeton to sit.

"Did Miss Rangaswamy tell you she practiced some

Ayurvedic healing massage on Christopher? She said it gets the energies flowing again."

"It did relieve some of his tight muscles. That will bring blood flowing to the area and be a healing benefit."

"I am so glad she thought to do that, then. I believe we have much to learn from the medical practices in India and other countries."

"I was approached by the East India Company to go to India for a couple of years as a company doctor. It was tempting for all the things I might learn; however, I have a good practice in London and did not want to jeopardize all the effort I'd already made in developing my practice. I decided—not without some regret—I shall learn from those that go instead of me," he said.

Cecilia smiled. "I'm sure your London patients appreciate your decision."

Dot came in then with the tea tray, and Cecilia served Dr. Seeton and herself.

"I must tell you, Lady Branstoke," Dr. Seeton said as he accepted the teacup from her, "I am impressed with the neck brace your housekeeper fashioned for young Sedgewick."

"Was he wearing it this morning?"

"Miss Rangaswamy put it on him to show me. It does all that I could want it to do to keep a young child from moving his head around. He didn't like it, but when I told him with the brace on, he could get out of bed for meals and could sit up for visits, he decided it was okay. I strictly said no running or jumping or other wild movements that young children are happy to make."

Cecilia sighed with relief. "That is good news. How long do you think we should keep him quiet and wearing the brace?"

"I'd like to see him wear the brace for a week; however, if after my visit tomorrow he shows continual improvement, he will not need to be bed-bound. I told Miss Rangaswamy she could continue with therapeutic massages. With your permission, I would ask her to teach me her techniques."

"I am delighted! But you do not need to ask my permission. That will be up to Miss Rangaswamy. It is her knowledge to share or not."

He bowed his head in acknowledgement. "I see," he said. "So I assume if I would like to know how to fashion a brace as your housekeeper did, I should speak directly to her?"

Cecilia nodded. "I pay wages for the work people do for me. I do not own their talents."

"You are unusual, then, Lady Branstoke."

She shrugged. "I do not hold that as a bad thing to be."

He smiled. "I would happen to agree with you, my lady."

~

"Thank you for seeing me, Mr. Partridge," James said as a young clerk showed him into Damon Partridge's office.

Damon Partridge rose from behind his desk and reached across to shake James's hand. "I admit your visit piqued my curiosity, Sir James." He gestured for James to sit in the chair in front of the desk as he sat down again.

James nodded. "That is understandable." He sat down and crossed one leg over the other as he settled into the chair.

"To what do I owe this visit? Do you foresee problems with the Waddley acquisition by my father?"

James waved a hand negligently. "I do not get involved in Waddley business. I leave that to my wife, Mr. Thornbridge, the solicitors, and the banks."

"Yes, I was surprised to see you did not assume ownership on your marriage."

James smiled lazily at Partridge, his eyes half hooded. One side of his lips kicked upward. "Lady Branstoke is much mistaken by society."

Damon Partridge looked at him consideringly. "Hmmm. Unknown depths. I wonder if I should warn my father."

James laughed. "My wife is eager to shed Waddley's. I have not seen the papers; however, knowing her feelings, I assume they are more than fair." His expression shifted to a serious mien. He shifted forward. "That is a part of the events in her life she wishes to put behind her."

Damon Partridge nodded. "No need to say more. I had Waddley's investigated for my father. He would not have made an offer without fully understanding the history of Waddley's, along with the state of the ledgers. The name will be changed immediately on signing the papers."

James' expression relaxed. "I'm glad we understand each other. But I did not come here today to discuss Waddley's. I'd like to learn about Paradise Medicinals."

A closed, shuttered expression took over Partridge's face. "What is it you want to know? I can tell you it is not taking any more investors at this time. How did you come to hear about Paradise?"

"Indirectly through Owen Sedgewick."

"Indirectly?"

"Six months ago Sedgewick thought he was dying, so he put his son and his son's nursemaid aboard a ship for England and entrusted the nursemaid with a packet of papers. With Soothcoor up north, she gave me those papers to see if they could provide any clue as to why someone would want to kidnap Sedgewick's son."

"Kidnap Christopher?" Damon exclaimed, leaning forward.

"You know of Sedgewick's son?"

"I was in India when he was learning to walk. He was the joy of the Sedgewicks."

"You say 'the Sedgewicks'—you believe they were married?"

"I *know* they were. Sedgewick showed me the marriage certificate. Said he couldn't brute it about because of Company rules and all." He waved his hand and scowled. "But tell me about Christopher and Sedgewick. You say Christopher is kidnapped and Sedgewick is dead?"

"Christopher has been recovered, and regarding Sedgewick, we don't know that for sure; however, I believe we can assume he is dead. His physician in India told him he did not have long to live, which is why he sent Christopher and Miss Rangaswamy to England."

"Rani Rangaswamy?"

"Yes."

Damon Partridge rose and walked to a cabinet on the side of the room. He drew out a bottle of brandy and held it out toward James.

"Yes, I will have some."

Partridge brought the bottle and two glasses back to the desk. He poured out the brandy and handed a glass to James. "I suggest you guard her well," he said as he poured a glass for himself. He took a sip and sat down. "That woman is Paradise Medicinals."

James, about to take a drink, placed both feet on the floor and lowered his hand to place the glass on the desk. Anything he might have expected Damon Partridge to say went out of his thoughts. He stared at the man across the desk. "Explain."

Partridge took in a deep breath and let it out slowly. "Rani, or Miss Rangaswamy, as you know her, was trained in Ayurvedic medicine by her aunt, who was a noted healer in Bombay."

"The only family relations she has talked about is her uncle and her cousin. She seemed to have revered her uncle."

"Yes, she did, for he rescued her from an orphanage when her mother died, and her father couldn't be bothered with her."

"Do you know who her father is? Miss Rangaswamy does not."

"Yes. Owen Sedgewick knew, as he investigated her before he brought her into his household, particularly as her cousin had a reputation as a wastrel. He had a long conversation with her uncle, who has repudiated worldly goods."

"Yes, Miss Rangaswamy told us about her uncle.

"It was from him, the uncle, that Sedgewick learned of Miss Rangaswamy's Ayurvedic knowledge."

"I see. Mr. Partridge, would you consider dining with us tonight? I would my wife hear all of this directly."

"I should be delighted to meet Lady Branstoke."

"And she you, as well. We are not keeping city hours. If you could come at, say six o'clock?"

"I can do that."

"Miss Rangaswamy is staying at our townhouse until Soothcoor returns to town."

"Hmm. You may want to warn her I am coming. If you did not know of her Ayurvedic knowledge, she might be keeping it hidden for a reason."

James cocked his head. "Why is that?"

"Fear."

James looked at him closely.

Damon Partridge compressed his lips. "You're

telling me Sedgewick was dying did not come as a surprise. I received a letter over a month ago—so that would have been on a ship that left before the ship Rani and Christopher came on—that he feared someone was trying to slowly poison him. He knew Rani would be blamed. He told me in the letter if he got worse, he would send her and Kit—his nickname for Christopher—to England. When you said Christopher came with his nursemaid, I did not immediately connect that person with Rani as she was so much more to the household, and there was another woman who took care of Christopher. I would wager Sedgewick told her his concerns and warned her not to share her knowledge openly."

James considered all that Partridge told him. "I understand. All the more reason for you to come tonight. Would you object if I also invite the Bow Street agent who is looking into Christopher's kidnapping? He believes Christopher is still in danger. From what you say, we need to be concerned for Miss Rangaswamy as well."

"If what I know can benefit Bow Street and keep Christopher and Rani safe, then by all means, invite him."

"Thank you." James rose. "Until tonight then."

James left Damon Partridge's office with his mind swirling with questions. There were greater implications to Christopher's kidnapping than just an earldom. He remembered Cecilia's restlessness earlier in the month. There could be no restlessness now.

# CHAPTER FIFTEEN

"**S**hould you like me to read more to you tomorrow?" Cecilia asked Christopher as she closed the book.

Christopher moved his eyes toward her, as that was all he could do within the brace Mrs. Dunstan created. "Yes, please."

Cecilia smiled. "I know you are frustrated wearing that brace, but if you continue to improve as you have, perhaps Dr. Seeton will allow you to take it off more. He was well pleased with your progress. Astonished even, I'd say."

"Yes, yes," said Rani. "So he tell me, too."

Cecilia looked over at Rani where she sat in the rocking chair she'd dragged in from her bedroom. "And did he tell you he thought it was your massage that helped?"

"No! Did he say so?"

"He did," Cecilia said, nodding. "He was impressed with your knowledge of therapeutic massage, as he called it. He was wondering if you could teach him. I told him that was up to you, not me."

A look of fear crossed her face, then she looked down. "No, I do not think so. I am but a learner."

Cecilia looked at her with concern. It appeared James's summation might be true. Owen did tell her to hide her talents. She sighed. She would not be happy then with what she next had to tell her.

"Miss Rangaswamy, do you know Mr. Damon Partridge?"

She looked up warily. She hesitated. "Yes," she finally said, in a quiet voice.

Cecilia nodded. "You have nothing to be afraid of. Mr. Partridge is concerned for you."

She looked at her like a deer about to flee into the woods. Her dark brown eyes were large and haunted.

Cecilia sighed. "Come, let us go to my parlor to talk." She turned back to Christopher. "It is time for you to take a nap. Sleep is healing, and we want you to heal quickly."

He protested, but Rani gently scolded him, and he settled down again. Then Rani followed Cecilia out of the room and down the hall to her sitting room.

"My lady, I—" Rani began, anguish in her voice.

"Shush. It is all right," Cecilia told her gently. She led her to her sofa and sat her down beside her. "Now, I will tell you what James learned today, and you can tell me what you will or won't. I shall not demand anything of you. Do you understand?"

Rani nodded, her expression sad, but resigned. Cecilia patted her hand.

"In the papers you let Sir James and me read, there was mention of an investment in a company called Paradise Medicinals."

Rani looked up, her eyes wide.

"Yes," Cecilia said. "James asked his solicitor to get more information about Paradise Medicinals and discovered two other people involved, one being the Earl of Soothcoor, and the other, Mr. Damon Partridge. With Soothcoor not yet in London, James went to visit

Mr. Partridge today. Mr. Partridge told him that *you* are Paradise Medicinals, that the plans for the company are nothing without you. He told James you are a talented Ayurvedic practitioner and that it is your skills that have provided Owen Sedgewick's relief from arthritis."

Rani bit her lip a moment, then nodded. "I am sorry to lie to you." Tears rolled down her cheeks. "But Sahib, he say to tell others it was Memsahib who created medicine. Memsahib had some little knowledge. I have more. When Sahib get sick, he try to hide it from me. I want to help, but he not let me. I don't know why. I talk to him many times, but he not take any medicine from me," she said, shaking her head sadly.

"Mr. Partridge told Sir James that Owen was afraid you would be accused of poisoning him. He sent a letter to Mr. Partridge saying this, about a month before he forced you to leave."

"Oh! But who would do that?"

"We don't know. You can expect all of us to be asking you questions to see if we can push your memory to bring more details forward. Do not be angry with us."

She shook her head, then wiped her eyes with her handkerchief. "No, I understand. I will not."

"Good," Cecilia said, giving Rani's hand a squeeze. "Why don't you rest before dinner. I'll send Dorothy to sit with Christopher for a while."

Rani nodded. "Yes, yes. I need to rest, to meditate. So much. It is all so much."

Cecilia rose and Rani stood as well. "Thank you, Lady Branstoke."

"For what?"

"For being nice to me, and not angry for not telling all truth."

Cecilia laughed. "You are an easy person to be nice

to. And how can I be angry when you were fulfilling your employer's instructions? Now go on to your room to rest. We will see you at dinner."

~

"MR. MARTIN, Mr. Thornbridge, thank you for coming to dinner on short notice," James told the gentlemen when they arrived. After the footman took their coats, James led them to his library.

"Your note said you have discovered someone with information about Mr. Sedgewick's business affairs that has relevance to this case," Lewis said.

"Yes. Gentlemen, please take a seat. I expect our other guest to be here momentarily. Can I get you a drink? Brandy?"

Lewis and David accepted, and James got out the cut-glass brandy decanter and glasses. "You remember Miss Rangaswamy had a packet of papers?" James asked as he poured the brandy.

"Yes," Lewis replied. "And you were going to look them over for any clues."

James nodded. He passed out the brandy glasses.

"When I went through them, I saw a few mentions of Paradise Medicinals. I asked my solicitor's office to see what more they could find out about this venture. This morning they brought me the names of the princi-pals." He sipped his drink. "The Earl of Soothcoor, Owen Sedgewick, and Damon Partridge."

"Damon Partridge?" David repeated.

"Yes, the same Damon Partridge whose father is purchasing Waddley Spice and Tea."

Lewis drew out a small notebook from his vest pocket, along with a pencil. Frowning, he flipped through his book. "Billy, Peasey's apprentice, said his master told him he could scout all of London for work;

however, he was to stay away from *the pear tree*. I asked him what that meant and he said, '*You know, from Mr. Partridge.*' I didn't ask which one or why." He ran his hand through his hair. "Damnation! Why did I not follow up on that?"

"There was no reason for you to tie the Damon Partridge or anyone in his family to this case. Regardless, this indicates Mr. Peasey knows more than he admitted to," James said.

"Yes, it does," Lewis said slowly.

"Excuse me, Sir James," interrupted Charwood from the doorway. "Mr. Partridge has arrived."

"Please bring him here to the library and inform Lady Branstoke."

"Very good, sir."

"Welcome, Mr. Partridge," James said, when Charwood showed him into the library. "Please come in."

Mr. Martin and Mr. Thornbridge rose from their seats.

"You know Mr. David Thornbridge already." James paused as the men exchanged greetings. "And this gentleman is Mr. Lewis Martin from Bow Street."

After those gentlemen exchanged greetings, James invited Damon to sit and handed him a glass of brandy.

"Your revelation to me this morning has thrown our original theory regarding the motivation for Christopher's kidnapping in disarray," James told Mr. Partridge.

"How so?" Damon asked.

Lewis Martin shifted in his seat and leaned forward. "We assumed this was somehow related to the Earl of Soothcoor dignities, as currently Owen Sedgewick is the Earl's heir if the Earl never marries and has children. That would make Christopher the Earl after his father, if he is legitimate and that can be proved."

"He is legitimate. I can vouch for that. I have seen the marriage lines," Damon said.

"That is good; however, your word could be called into question," Lewis said.

"I don't know why. It is not as if I had anything to gain by making that up."

"I understand," Lewis said.

Damon scratched the side of his head. "But who's in line after Owen, if Christopher is declared not legitimate?"

"Charles Sedgewick, Owen's half-brother."

"What kind of man is he?"

"A London dandy, always ready for a party, a card game, or running from his creditors," James said. "But he is a congenial fellow. Never had any hope or expectations for the title that I am aware of, though Owen told everyone he would never have children, as he did not want any child to suffer as he has suffered."

"But he did marry and had a child," Damon said.

"The Dowager Countess, his stepmother, does not believe he married. As her two youngest sons are in India now, they have never written anything to her about Owen being married."

Damon nodded. "They may not know. Owen and I had many long talks when I was in India four years ago. He confided in me about his marriage, showed me the document. He did not want it known, as The East India Company frowned on such marriages."

"Yes," James said, "After the Kirkpatrick marriage and his adoption of Indian manners and ways."

"Precisely," Damon said. "They would find ways to 'punish' a man for taking an Indian spouse. Promotion opportunities disappeared, men were transferred to the least favorable locations—that sort of retribution."

"I was under the impression that he married his

consort because she gave him the medicine that alleviated his pain," James said.

"That's partially correct," Damon said. "Sushmita Dhar had some knowledge of Ayurvedic medicine, particularly knowledge about Kalihari."

"Kalihari?" Lewis asked, as he jotted the name in his occurrence book.

"Yes, it is a vine that produces a flower that looks like a candle flame. In my research, I've seen it described as a Flame Lily. Very intriguing to see. It is also highly poisonous."

"How can a poisonous plant also be a medicine?" Lewis asked.

"Like foxglove," David said. "That's poisonous, but a knowledgeable herbalist can create a medicine for heart ailments with it."

Lewis nodded. "I'd forgotten about that plant."

The door to the library opened. Cecilia came in smiling, her eyes dancing. "Come, my dear," she said to Rani behind her. Rani followed her in. All the gentlemen rose.

Rani wore a beautifully simple, midnight-blue saree, with a thin silver-woven edge, and small, embroidered silver stars spaced across the fabric like stars in the sky. Cecilia was delighted to note the gentlemen's reactions.

James only raised an eyebrow; however, the other three gentlemen stood straighter.

"Cecilia, this gentleman is Damon Partridge. Damon, allow me to present my wife, Lady Cecilia Branstoke."

Damon stepped toward her to take her hand in his. "Delighted, my lady," he said.

"Miss Rangaswamy," James continued, "I believe you know all these gentlemen."

"Yes, yes." She curtsied.

"Cecilia, your timing is perfect. Mr. Partridge was starting to tell us about a plant called Kalihari."

Rani's head flew up, and she stared first at James, then at Mr. Partridge, her eyes wide and uncertain.

"It is all right, Rani," assured Damon. "There is no need to be afraid. You are with friends."

"Yes, you are," said Cecilia, coming up beside Rani and wrapping her arm around her back. Cecilia looked at the gentlemen. "Dinner is waiting. We can continue this discussion after dinner, when we adjourn to the parlor. No sitting in the dining room afterward while you blow a cloud or something."

James laughed, and taking their cue from him, the other gentlemen did as well.

Cecilia kept the dinner conversation light, not allowing any digression into the mystery they resolved to unravel. She did allow Rani to answer questions about her childhood in India and her aunt's knowledge in ayurveda.

"Ayurveda is—hmm—the knowledge of life," she said softly.

Cecilia noted how her eyes shown and her face lit from within when she spoke of the practice.

"We believe disease come from imbalances within." She wobbled her hands like a scale out of balance. "And from the stress one feels in here." She laid a hand against her heart. "We administer herbs in special formulas for different conditions, make oils to rub on the body, give massages—all manner of tools to help a person regain their internal balance," she said.

Cecilia knew Miss Rangaswamy had asked Mrs. Dunstan what she could do in England. Since she had a passion for this Indian form of medicine, perhaps there was something in ayurveda she could do to stay within her passion. Cecilia decided she would help her in whatever way she could.

Discussion and questions around the table about Ayurvedic practices fascinated everyone, so the meal passed quickly. Cecilia directed the footmen to serve dessert in the parlor with tea, coffee, and brandy.

Once everyone had been served, Cecilia brought the conversation back to the mystery.

"Mr. Partridge, what were your and Owen's and Soothcoor's plans for Paradise Medicinals?"

"We wanted to bring some of the best of Ayurvedic medicines and traditions to England. You have heard how Owen suffered from his arthritis. He thought if he could bring some relief to others who suffered, it would be profitable."

"But, but—" interrupted Rani, fairly jumping out of her seat on the sofa.

"Yes, I know, Rani. The best relief Owen received was with medications you customized for him. We cannot hope to give everyone the same medicine and see the same results."

"No, and what is good for Sahib may harm another person." She shook her head, "It is not easy just to say *take this medicine.*'"

"I know Rani. But there are other medicines that can be given to everyone. Like some of your oils."

She reluctantly nodded her head.

"And isn't the dosage of Kalihari that Sushmita originally gave to Owen, a dosage that could work at some extent for all?"

"Yes."

"To provide more than that basic relief needs a custom touch. Sushmita knew that, and that is why she began looking for you when she discovered your aunt had passed," Damon went on.

"I thought Miss Rangaswamy was hired as a nurse-maid," said James.

"She was, *and* as an Ayurvedic practitioner. Sushmita's brother had been one of Abhijt Rangaswamy's students, so Sushmita asked him to help locate Rani. When her brother learned Rani had been turned out by Manjo Rangaswamy, Sushmita decided to offer her the position of a nursemaid when they found her, and Owen would not deny her." Damon turned to Rani. "How did they find you? I don't think I ever heard that part."

Rani laughed and clapped her hands together. "It was an accident! I was walking out of the rectory, still talking to Mrs. Crane, the rector's wife. I walked backward as I talked and ran into Atul Dhar. He started to yell at me but stopped when he recognized me from his school days. He grabbed me up and swung me around, ecstatic to find me. He explained to Mrs. Crane and me that his sister was looking for me, and would I consider coming to work for her.

Mrs. Crane told me to seek it out, for she reminded me the Lord works in mysterious ways. I did, and Sushmita and I became close friends, not master and servant."

"How did Sushmita die?" James asked. Lewis looked at him sharply.

Rani's eyes became unfocused. She shook her head. "I don't know," she said slowly.

"You don't know?" Damon repeated, staring at her.

She looked at him and shook her head again. "You know she was sickly. She had the asthma. But she had been better, much stronger. Then she gets sick in her stomach. It wasn't anything I knew, but I suspected, as did Sahib, that she was being poisoned. We could not find the source; we could not prove anything. He replaced all the servants, everyone, and for a time, she got a little better. But then she got her asthma again, and with the two attacking her, she had not strength to fight both, and in the night, she go to sleep and not wake up." Tears sparkled in her eyes. She bit her lower lip.

"Did anyone visit the house before or during Mrs. Sedgewick's illness?" Lewis asked.

Rani thought, then shrugged and shook her head. "Company people. Mainly English doctor I did not like and his younger brother, who worked for Sahib at the company. I did not like him either." Her lip curled up.

"What was it about them you did not like?"

"The Doctor, he hold up his head and look down his nose. Always, like we are not worth being around. But he was always asking about the medicine Sahib take for his arthritis. He wanted to talk to who made it. Sahib lied, he say traveling person. He would be back in three months and he'd get more then. This doctor wants to take what Sahib have. He told him *no*, as he would not have medicine. Doctor not happy. Says he is leaving India within the month. Wants to study India medicine. Sahib tells him he knows medicine is made from a plant in our yard. Tells doctor he can take some specimens back to England. I speak up then, I say all parts are poisonous, but mainly the root. He stare at me a moment and I'm afraid. I don't know why."

"Can you describe him?" James asked.

"Hmm—Tall, but not as tall as Mr. Partridge, but same shoulders, same, same," she said, with her hands indicating a trim body type. "Black hair with gray he wear combed back with something on it. It is oily looking. Long face, gray beard, gray mustache. Nose is like a blade, and he stares down it with gray eyes. Gray man, even clothes are gray."

"James, her description sounds like Dr. Lakewood!" Cecilia said.

"Yes, yes," Rani said. "That is it! I forget before. That is name. And brother is Frederick."

Lewis and David looked surprised. Damon frowned. "How did you know?"

"Cecilia and I met him two nights ago at Lady Amblethorpe's musical. He was in the company of the Dowager Countess of Soothcoor. She has been allowing him the use of her conservatory for his plants that he brought back from India," James said.

"Owen did write to me about a doctor who was in India who was interested in the possibility for Kalihari," Damon said.

"Did he want to bring this gentleman into your venture?"

Damon laughed harshly. "Hardly. He did not like the man. Said he treated his sister at one time and wanted to trade on that acquaintance to get closer to Owen and knowledge of how Kalihari worked. Kept pestering him about it, and as Rani said, wanted to take Owen's medication from him."

"Interesting," Lewis said. He looked down at his book, then up, his eyes narrowed.

"What is it?" James asked.

"Let me read a note I took from the lad who saw Peasey buy Christopher's apprenticeship: *Tall. Tall man. Way tall*—remember this is one of the street lads speaking. *Beard. Big shoulders but not fat. Long coat. Gray, not black in lamp light. Too neat.*"

"James, that does sound a lot like the man we saw," Cecilia said.

"Yes, but it is not evidence."

"He is right, Lady Branstoke," Lewis said. "I cannot do anything directly with this information, but it does give us a direction for further investigation."

The bell rang at the door, followed by heavy thudding against the wood.

"Soothcoor!" James said, as he got to his feet and ran toward the front door. Everyone ran behind him. Nate was already opening the door. The moment he lifted the latch, the door was pushed open and flung him aside. He stumbled and fell. Lewis helped him up.

The Earl of Soothcoor was disheveled and dirty. He didn't wear a hat, and his shoulder-length, gray-streaked black hair stood up in wild disarray. He breathed heavily.

"What's the news?" he gasped out, grabbing on to James.

"We have him. He's safe, Alastair."

"Safe?"

"Yes, safe. We rescued him yesterday."

"Thank God!" He slid out of James's hand to sit on the floor. "Thank God," he said again. He looked up at everyone around him. "Can someone see to my horse? The creature is nigh dead on her feet."

# CHAPTER SIXTEEN

Cecilia laughed while tears ran down her cheeks. "Of course! Nate?"

"Yes, my lady, immediately," the young footman said. He threaded his way through everyone in the hall to get to the door and quietly closed it behind him as he went out.

James leaned over to help the Earl back to his feet. Soothcoor staggered, almost too tired to stand. Damon got on the other side of him to offer support.

"Let's get you to a room, and I'll have a tray brought to you," Cecilia said.

"No," he said, his breathing still labored. "Must see Christopher first. Must see my nephew."

"I understand," said James. "Mr. Partridge?"

"Of course, Sir James."

James and Damon half carried, half led Soothcoor to the nursery. Rani ran ahead of them. From a sideboard in the hall, she lit a candle. She quietly opened the nursery door and motioned with her finger for all to be quiet. She walked toward the bed and held the candle aloft so Soothcoor could see Christopher.

Tears ran down Soothcoor's cheeks. "Thank you," he whispered, and turned away to signal James and

Damon to take him out of the room. Rani indicated she would stay with Christopher.

"I'm afraid you will have to help him up one more flight," Cecilia whispered to James and Damon. "It will be the first room on the left.

They nodded. "Cecilia, send my man up, please," James said grimly. He'd never seen Soothcoor in such an exhausted state. He might have to have Dr. Seeton see to him in the morning, as well as Christopher. He couldn't imagine how Soothcoor had gotten back to London so fast. Time for revelations and stories on the morrow. He was here, and they had to make sure he recovered. Blast the man! Killing himself wouldn't help Christopher. He frowned as he and Damon carried the exhausted man up the stairs.

After sending James's valet to Soothcoor's room, Cecilia joined David and Lewis in the entry hall and escorted them back to the library.

"I think I could use a brandy now," she said on a deep breath. "Anyone else?"

Lewis and David chuckled and agreed.

"Allow me," David said, getting clean glasses out of the small hutch between the windows. He poured brandy for Cecilia and Lewis.

Fifteen minutes later, James and Damon joined them. David rose to pour them brandies.

"Thank you," James said, as he settled on the sofa next to his wife. "We can expect Charles here tomorrow," he told her. He turned toward the others. "At the last change of horses, Charles was too tired to go on. Soothcoor feared he would fall asleep and slide off his mount. He convinced him to take a room and follow along in the morning. Soothcoor felt he was too close to wait another day, so he pushed his horse and himself to get here."

"Once he saw Christopher, whatever will power

he'd been using to keep going burned away, like burning the last bit of oil in a lamp snuffs the light." Damon said.

"I hope he sleeps late, now that he knows Christopher is safe." Cecilia said.

"He won't," James said. "He'll be awake with the first light to make sure what he saw last night was real. Then he'll want to be on the hunt."

Lewis set his brandy glass on the side table. "I'd best be leaving, then. I'd like to see what I can learn about this Dr. Lakewood. And speak to Mr. Peasey as well. I'll return in the morning to speak with Lord Soothcoor."

David and Damon set their glasses down and rose, saying they too would be back in the morning, each man wanting to be included in the hunt.

Cecilia and James saw them to the entry and waited with them as Nate retrieved their coats and hats.

As they turned to leave, Lewis turned back, frowning. "This isn't over. I feel that in my gut."

"We won't be complacent, Mr. Martin," James promised.

Lewis nodded and left.

~

CECILIA TOOK a small sip of sherry as she studied the fichu she'd been embroidering, studying each side to ensure the design on one side was a mirror of the opposite side. She had a missing vine and some French knots yet to do, but it was almost done. She felt pleased with her work. She lacked the needlework skills and the patience of many of her peers. However, she had been improving. She might even try embroidery next on a larger field than a fichu. Perhaps a spring jacket sleeve, she mused. A light-weight pelisse in an apple green, perhaps.

She set her sewing aside and took another sip of sherry. She was too restless to seek her bed yet. Besides, it was early still, the clock on the mantel only chiming nine times within the last ten minutes. She glanced over at her husband, who sat in a chair next to the fireplace, reading.

He must have felt her regard, for he looked up at her. He set his book aside. Cecilia got up from the sofa and walked over to him. He held out his arms, and she slid onto his lap, laying her head on his shoulder. He wrapped his arms around her.

"Remember last week at Summerworth Park, how restless you were?" he asked.

"Hmm."

"Bored with our quiet life in the country," he teased.

She raised her head at that. "Our quiet life did not bore me!" she protested.

"You were bored," he asserted.

She shrugged. "Maybe a little."

"Have the events of the last few days satisfied you for a while?"

"James," she protested, "You make me sound like some sort of disaster addict." She picked at a piece of fluff on his jacket.

"My love, after years of living in a gilded cage, you have too much living to make up for."

"Is that how it seems to you? That I am making up for years of inactivity?" she asked, with slightly feigned petulance.

"It does."

She relented and smiled softly. "I can see there is truth to that. I was hoping to be expecting a child by now."

"I know. If it happens, that will be wonderful. If it doesn't, so be it. I am—"

Loud, rapid pounding resounded against the front door.

"What?" Cecilia said, as she rose from James's lap. He rose after her, and they hurried across the parlor.

They opened the parlor door as Charwood opened the front door.

"You are supposed to use the back entrance," they heard Charwood reprimand.

"We has ta see Sar James and his missus!" cried out a young male voice.

"Yeah, 'tis urgent," said another

Charwood pushed the door against them.

"Charwood, what are you about? Let them in!" Sir James said, striding forward.

"Thank ye, sar," said Daniel Wrightson, ducking under Charwood's arm. Billy followed close behind.

Both boys were out of breath.

"We couldna find Mr. Martin," said Daniel, huffing, breathless as he talked. "'Tweren't at his lodgin' ner Bow Street, so we came ta ya, sar."

"What is it?" James asked. He grasped them by their shoulders.

"'Tis Mr. Peasey, sar," said Billy, looking up at him, his voice cracking. James could feel his body quivering under his hand.

"Poisoned," Daniel supplied dramatically, rolling his eyes and falling to the floor.

"Poisoned?" echoed Cecilia.

"Bloody hell," swore Sir James.

Daniel scrambled to his feet.

Cecilia came forward, lightly touching one boy, then the other with reassurance.

"Let's go to my library," James said, after taking in their dirty attire. "Charwood, some refreshments for the boys. I think they've had a traumatic night."

"Yes, sar," said Billy reverently. "I ain't never seen a man die like that afore."

Cecilia led them to the library and had the boys sit down by the desk. James pulled a chair up for Cecilia from the card table, then leaned against the edge of his desk.

"Now tell us everything," Cecilia said.

"Yes, your Ladyship," said Billy. His brows drew together as he shuddered slightly. He leaned forward. "Mr. Peasey, he went to da pub like his usual--and 'ticularly when he gets in the fidgets and be worrin'. When he come back to da house, he was in a good mood and even had a pail of beer that he said his friend bought for him as he was leaving."

"Does this friend have a name?" James asked.

Billy shook his head. "Never said no name, don't know who this friend were, but he met him nigh every night fer da past week," said Billy.

Daniel nodded. "I seed him many times walk'n to en frum," Daniel added.

Billy nodded. "I were glad 'cause that meant he warn't going ta beat me agin for losin' Tristan."

"His name is Krishan, and you didn't lose Krishan," Cecilia said, smiling. "We took him."

"But I tol' ya he look'd like dat paper picture. Mr. Peasey said I shoulda lied."

"I probably wouldn't have believed you if you tried to lie," Cecilia said, smiling. "Your face would have given you away."

He nodded morosely.

"But tell us about Mr. Peasey," James said.

Billy swallowed and nodded. "As I said, he had a pail of beer. Talked about da gent who bought him the beer, said he'd get his blunt back to him. Right gentlemanly, and how everything was a misunderstandin'."

Charwood entered quietly with refreshments. James

motioned him to wait a moment so as not to disrupt Billy's story.

"I asked how there could be a misunderstandin' about a gentry boy. He laughed and toll me not ta wor-rit, jest find him a replacement. He leaned back in his chair, all smiles as he drank him his beer. Drank all of it. Then he says he don't feel too good."

Billy's face contorted, his lips flattened, and his nos-trils flared. "It were awful. He started retching, and then shittin' his pants. I wanted to run but, he tol' me to stay."

Cecilia, wide-eyed, had her hand over her mouth as she listened in horror. Billy's eyes stared unseeing be-fore him, seeing only the memory. "Then he went quiet like fer a bit," he said, "and I were tryin' to clean up. He whispered his legs were dead. I had to lean close to him to hear him. He smelled like death, but he were still alive. He knowed he were dying. Cursed that beer and the fancy man wot gave it him. He started shakin' all over, his back archin', screamin'!"

Billy placed his hands over his ears as if to stop hearing the memory. Tears streamed down his face. "It were awful. He started up to retch agin. Blood wit bub-bles. He grabbed mi hand tight and fell back. Then his eyes rolled, and he were dead." He shook his head. "That quick," he whispered. "I had to pry mi fing'rs loose."

The crash of the refreshments tray hitting the floor stirred them all out of the horror stupor they'd fallen into listening to Billy.

Charwood stood over the mess, shaking, his face white. He looked at Sir James. "I killed her," he whispered.

James grabbed his arm. "What are you saying? Killed who?"

"The Indian woman," Charwood breathed.

"No!" Cecilia screamed. She grabbed on to Charwood's other arm, shaking him.

"Cecilia, stop," ordered James. "Charwood, what did you do?"

"He gave me this orange powder, said if I put it in her drink, it would make her silly and forgetful, and you'd get a disgust for her. So I put it in hot chocolate and took it to her."

Cecilia ran up the stairs and down the hall to the nursery. Behind her followed James and the two boys. Rani was not in the nursery. Cecilia opened her bedroom door without knocking. She collapsed against the door when she saw Rani in her nightgown, sitting on the edge of her bed, brushing her hair.

"You didn't drink it?" Cecilia asked, breathless.

Behind her stood James, with the boys peering around him.

"Drink what?" Rani asked, confused.

"Hot chocolate. Charwood said he brought you hot chocolate."

"Yes, yes. I do not drink it." Rani wrinkled her nose. "I do not like hot chocolate. Why? What is this?" she asked, looking at their faces.

"Charwood said he added a dark orange powder to it. We think it may have been poison. Where is the cup?"

"Dark orange?" Rani got up and pushed past them. "I say to Dot she could have it. She was going to the kitchen to heat again. We must stop her!" She ran down the servants' stairs to the kitchen.

Dot sat at the table, the cup of chocolate hovering near her lips.

"Stop! Don't drink!" Rani yelled.

Cecilia swept past her and knocked the cup from Dot's hand, then swept the chocolate pot and saucer from the table as well, to shatter on the fitted stone floor.

"Did you drink?" Rani asked.

"A little, a couple of sips," Dot answered, bewildered.

"Don't move, do nothing. I be back," Rani ordered. She ran back up the stairs.

"What's going on?" Dot asked.

Cecilia put her arm around her. "There may have been poison in that chocolate. We don't know for sure."

"I don't want to die," Dot cried, clinging to Cecilia.

"I am hoping, by the way Miss Rangaswamy ran off, she has an antidote," James said grimly. He looked at the boys who had followed them. "Go back to the library and watch over Charwood. Don't let him leave."

"Yes, sir," said Daniel. "Come on, Billy. Mr. Martin will want to talk to Mr. Charwood."

Rani met them on the stairs, almost knocking Daniel over with the satchel she held. She brought it into the kitchen and turned it over on the table, searching through the contents of vials and packets. "Water, please," she said as she picked up a box tied with twine. She slipped off the twine and opened the box. Inside were dried hot peppers. She angrily muttered something in her own language and opened another box. It contained charcoal. She grabbed up a handful and crushed it over the mug of water Cecilia had set before her.

Cecilia grabbed a wooden spoon from a sideboard and handed it to Rani. She stirred the charcoal and water together. She handed the mug to Dot. "Drink," she said.

Dot made a face and tried to push it away. "Drink!" Rani ordered, yelling. "Drink! Drink!" she said again.

Startled, Dot took the mug and drank.

"Drink it faster," Cecilia said. "I've read charcoal is

an antidote for poison if you drink it soon after you have swallowed the poison."

"Yes, yes," Rani nodded.

Dot's wide eyes looked at them over the rim of the mug as she drank the charcoal-laced water, her mouth soon rimmed with black.

"We do again," Rani said, when Dot finished the mug. James got the mug refilled with water for Rani while Cecilia comforted Dot.

"What now?" James asked as they watch Dot finish the second mug of charcoal and water. Cecilia handed her a towel to wipe the residual charcoal off her lips.

"We wait," Rani said.

Dot clenched the towel to her face and cried harder.

# CHAPTER SEVENTEEN

*T*he bell rang stridently.

"At this hour, I'd wager that is Mr. Martin," said James, walking toward the stairs.

Cecilia looked toward the stairs as James lightly ran up them, then over at Dot. She wanted to speak to the Bow Street agent and to Charwood again; however, she did not want to abandon her housemaid.

"If my lady could send Nate down to me, he can help me get Dot to her room," Rani said.

"Are you sure?"

"Yes, madam. I stay with her, watch her. Krishan sleeps through the night. But she be fine." She placed a hand on her heart. "In my heart, I know," she said solemnly.

"All right," Cecilia said. She felt guilty for leaving, but Rani would be of more benefit to Dorothy than she would.

"Nate, please go to the kitchen to help Rani take Dorothy to her room," Cecilia said when she reached the entrance hall.

"What happened to Dot?" he asked.

Cecilia had not realized that despite the flurry of excitement, not everyone knew what had been going on. "She drank some bad chocolate Mr. Charwood made for Miss Rangaswamy." When he looked like he had more questions, Cecilia cut him off. "Not now. Please, go assist Miss Rangaswamy."

"Yes, my lady," Nate said, and went down the hall to the stairs.

Cecilia walked to the library. Only one muffled voice came through the door. She leaned closer to the door, then smirked at herself. Why was she eavesdropping? She should just go in!

She pushed the double doors open as Billy finished telling Mr. Martin what had happened. She was glad to have missed a repeat of the gruesome details. It would hit her too hard to be reminded that might have been Dorothy's fate.

Everyone looked at her as she entered.

"How is she?" asked Lewis.

"Miss Rangaswamy gave her charcoal in water to fight the poison, but she doesn't believe she drank enough to poison her."

Lewis looked over to where Charwood sat in a chair by the desk, his shoulders slumped, his head down. "It looks like you will escape the hangman's noose, Mr. Charwood," he said brutally.

His head flew up. "I didn't know!" Charwood protested.

"You may not have intended to kill her, but you did intend her malicious harm," James said harshly. "My God, man, why?"

Mr. Charwood looked up, tears streaking his long face. "Because of my brother," he said brokenly.

"I don't understand," said Cecilia as she crossed the room to stand next to James. He wrapped his arm around her to pull her close to him.

Mr. Charwood sobbed and wiped his eyes with his handkerchief. "Chester was in the East India Army. He loved India. He made many Indian friends, but they killed him!"

"His friends killed him?" James asked.

"His best friend betrayed him to the Nepalese. Three days they tortured him before he died. My little brother," he said bitterly. "Those Indians cannot be trusted! My new friend Mr. Gray, who gave me the powder, has lived in India. He warns they are devious. Many of us discuss this at the pub together and agree."

"What does this Mr. Gray look like?" Lewis asked.

"Tall man. Neatly dressed like one of the city clerks. Wears gray a lot. When I teased him about the sameness of his attire, he laughed. Said, why not? His last name is Gray, and he had gray eyes, he says as he gets older his hair is going gray, as is his mustache and beard. Might as well dress all in gray. Said it was his own little joke."

"The Gray Man," Billy whispered.

"What's that?" James asked.

Billy looked over at him. "One time that be wot Mr. Peasey called him an' laughed. Said 'twer da best joke."

There was a tap on the parlor door, and Rani peeked in. "May I come in?" she asked.

"Of course," said James. "I take it Dorothy is resting?"

"Yes, yes. Nate, he say he would stay with her while I come down to talk to you. I have something to ask Mr. Charwood. Is it permitted?"

"Yes," Lewis said.

Rani dragged her arm from behind her to reveal she'd brought the satchel she'd taken the charcoal from. She set it on the table by the door and pulled out a packet. She carefully untied the string and unfolded the paper covering the contents. Inside the paper was a dull rusty brown fine powder. She brought it over by Mr. Charwood. "The powder you put in the chocolate, did it look like this?" she asked, extending her hand toward him.

Mr. Charwood looked at the powder. He nodded. "Yes, it looked like that."

Rani pulled the paper and its contents back, then proceeded to carefully rewrap the paper back into a neat package. "This is ground Kalihari tuber, where is most poison."

"Kalihari tuber?"

"Yes, it is also what I make medicine from that ease the arthritis. What we talk of yesterday." She looked at Mr. Charwood. "How much you put in chocolate?"

"Two teaspoons," he said wearily. "Mr. Gray said to use it all, two tablespoons, but I thought to give you less and have some for another time."

Rani looked up. "If she drank the entire cup, she maybe die, maybe not. But she only have two sips, she say, and we stop her before she drinks more." She inhaled and exhaled deeply. "I am happy. She will be fine." She looked at them all again. "I go back to be with her now."

She started to leave but paused and looked back. "I can make drawing of plant if needed."

"That would be beneficial," Lewis told her solemnly. "Thank you for coming down to clarify the poison and the quantity effect."

She nodded and left.

"Stand up, Mr. Charwood. You are going to the magistrate," said Lewis.

Charwood slowly rose to his feet, a broken man. Cecilia felt it hard not to feel a little sorry for him. She steeled her heart.

"Boys, come with me," Lewis instructed. "I'll need your help guarding this one," he said severely, though he winked at Cecilia.

"Mr. Martin," Cecilia said, coming up to him and

stilling him with a hand on his forearm. "What will be-come of Billy?"

"I have an idea that I think will meet with your ap-proval. We can discuss it tomorrow. In the meantime, he will be cared for, I promise."

"You are a good man. Thank you," she said, stepping away. She watched them leave with a heavy heart. It hurt that one of her servants could willfully harm an-other. But people were complex beings, and what leads one down a path of good and another down a path of jealously and vengeance is unknown.

THE EARL of Soothcoor was up and in the nursery when she entered in the morning to check on Christo-pher. He was making Christopher giggle with light tickling which, after last night's events, lightened her heart. She hadn't slept well but had clung to James in the night.

Watching them, Cecilia laughed. "Careful," she warned, though she smiled with delight at their play. She motioned him to stay sitting on the edge of the bed and not to get up on her account. "Dr. Seeton has not allowed movement yet. Though he said Christopher can get up for a little while today, so long as he wears his brace."

"The bandage on his head—Christopher tells me he was stuck in a chimney?" Soothcoor said quizzically, his brows furrowing with faint disbelief.

Cecilia nodded. Her lips compressed for a moment. "Yes, he was. Has he told you of his *adventure*? That is what he will think of it when he's older, though right now the memories are probably frightening."

"A little. I would like to hear of it from you and Sir James."

"We can tell you, but it really is Miss Rangaswamy's story."

He frowned. "And where is this woman? I expected her to be here, but the door to her room is ajar and she is not to be seen. Christopher said he hadn't seen her this morning. I can't like that."

Cecilia didn't want to say anything in front of Christopher. "She has been watching over one of the maids who became ill last night," she said carefully. "Miss Rangaswamy has some knowledge of the healing arts. At my request, she has been caring for her."

"So soon after Christopher's experience and injuries?" Soothcoor demanded.

She sighed heavily and leaned her head against the nursery door. "That is a story Sir James can tell you. I don't know that I can right now without crying."

He frowned as he looked at her. He rose from the bed. "Is it somehow related to Christopher's kidnapping?" he murmured, his back turned to Christopher.

She hesitated, then nodded.

"I see," he said heavily. His long face appeared longer, with concern etched on his features.

The door to the nursery opened and Rani entered. "I'm sorry, Krishan!" she called out before she saw Cecilia and the Earl in the room. She curtsied. "I will get Krishan washed and dressed now for breakfast."

"Can I go downstairs?" Krishan asked eagerly, looking from one face to another.

"Doctor say today, yes," Rani said.

Cecilia smiled at him. "Then we will wait breakfast for you. No need to hurry."

"Thank you, madam," Rani said.

"Is someone with Dorothy? How is she this morning?" Cecilia asked.

"Mrs. Dunstan is with her. She is unhappy we did not wake her to help last night. Nate told her all this morning. Dot is better. She retch one time only. She doesn't feel good, but she will be fine in a day or so."

"That is welcome news," Cecilia said. "Did you get any sleep last night?"

"Yes, yes. I sleep on floor next to her bed."

"On the floor!" Guilt, like a sea wave, crashed over Cecilia.

"Nate brought me blankets," Rani said almost absently, as she went over to Christopher and sat next to him.

Cecilia sighed. "I'm glad Nate thought to help you. I am sorry I did not think of that."

Rani smiled as she shrugged. "So much going on. But Dot will be fine. That is important thing."

Soothcoor looked from one woman to the other but didn't comment.

Cecilia nodded and opened the nursery door. She and Soothcoor left the room.

"Cecilia, what is going on?" Soothcoor quietly asked.

She shook her head. "We don't know the whole of it yet. We have ideas, but nothing seems to come together. Let me tell the staff to hold breakfast for Krishan—I mean Christopher, then we can join James in the library."

"I heard Miss Rangaswamy refer to him as Krishan. Owen, in his letters to me, called him Kit."

Cecilia agreed. "It is my understanding his mother, Miss Rangaswamy, and other servants in India called him Krishan. I have fallen into the habit of calling him Krishan, as Miss Rangaswamy does."

He nodded. "I will ask him what he wants me to call him."

She turned to look up at him. "That is kind of you. Nate," she said as they reached the entry. "Krishan will join us for breakfast. Please tell Cook and the staff to hold breakfast until he is dressed."

"Yes, my lady." Nate trotted down the hall to the stairs leading to the kitchen.

"The library is this way," Cecilia told the Earl.

When they entered the library, Cecilia saw Mr. Martin before them, seated at the desk. He rose when he saw them.

"Soothcoor!" James said, delighted to see his friend recovered. He came around the desk. He gripped Soothcoor's shoulders. "How are you today? No ill effects from your journey to get here? Did you sleep comfortably?"

"Yes, thank you. I am more at peace, especially now that I have spent some time with Christopher. But I admit I'm not as young as I used to be, and all parts of my body ache this morning. I don't wish to do that ride again, but I'm damn glad I did."

"Come and meet Mr. Lewis Martin," James said. "Mr. Martin is with Bow Street and was instrumental in our finding Christopher."

"Mr. Martin," Soothcoor said, shaking Lewis's hand and grabbing his arm with the other hand. "I can't thank you enough. When I got word from Mr. Thornbridge that Christopher was in the country but had been kidnapped, I felt the world collapse around me. Thank you."

"My lord, we worked together to effect a happy discovery. But as I was saying to Sir James, we are not at the end of this villainy. Are you acquainted with Dr. Jonathan Lakewood?"

"Yes," he replied easily. "My stepmother introduced me to him a few weeks ago. Reminded me he was the doctor who cared for my niece after her son, George, was born."

"I think we should all be seated," James said, leading

Cecilia to the sofa by the fireplace. Their guests took the chairs flanking the sofa.

Lewis leaned forward, hands clasped between his knees. "We suspect Dr. Lakewood to have involvement in the kidnapping of your nephew, the death of Mr. Percival Peasey, and an attempted murder of Miss Rani Rangaswamy," Lewis said heavily.

"Impossible," Soothcoor scoffed. He looked from Mr. Martin to the Branstokes. "That's ridiculous. He is trained to save lives, not take lives."

James shook his head. "Listen to Mr. Martin," he said. "We don't understand it either, but we agree with Mr. Martin." He looked at Lewis. "Please go ahead."

Lewis nodded. "Two months ago, a tall man in theatrical costume garb met with a couple of louts and offered them money to loiter around the East India Docks. They were to look for a ship with a young boy among the passengers. The costumed gentleman gave them a description of the child's eyes by which to identify him. They were told to ensure the child never made it to the Earl of Soothcoor. They were well-compensated for their time, with the promise of more later."

Soothcoor frowned and shook his head. "Go on."

"When they realized the boy they were waiting for had disembarked from a new ship in port, they paid a laundress named Muriel Patterson to kidnap the boy and promised her £5 for doing so."

Nate pushed the door open. "Since we have pushed breakfast back, Cook suggested you might like coffee or tea." He carried the tea tray over to the card table by the windows.

"Thank you, Nate, and give our thanks to Cook." Cecilia said. She rose from the sofa to pour out cups of coffee and tea. Cecilia asked what everyone wanted. Only Mr. Martin requested tea, James and Soothcoor preferring black coffee.

"This Patterson woman, have you arrested her?" Soothcoor asked.

Lewis tipped his head and sighed. He took his tea from Cecilia, then looked back at the Earl. "The men that hired her, killed her." He blew gently on his tea to cool it and took a sip. "They took Christopher to one of the rougher parts of London, locked him in an upstairs room with outside access at a tavern, and went back downstairs and into the tavern for a mug of ale to celebrate. While they were celebrating, a third party kidnapped the boy from them and sold him into apprenticeship to a chimney sweep."

"Egad! Why? How do you know all this?" Soothcoor asked.

"The *why*, we have yet to figure out. The *how* is through the friends I've made with the mudlark gangs and others. They are my eyes and ears in the city. I tell them not to get involved, just watch and report."

"Except young Daniel did get involved when he went to Mrs. Patterson after she was stabbed," Cecilia reminded him.

"Yes, and while I honor his intentions, as he didn't know how badly she was hurt, I told him not to do that again. At least not alone," Lewis said sternly. "I cannot stress enough to these runabouts how dangerous is their curiosity. I have befriended them for their safety as well as communication sources."

"But with all the chimney sweeps in the city, and as grimy as they remain, how did you find Christopher?"

"He has the puppy dog Sedgewick eyes," James dryly explained.

Cecilia laughed. "Yes, and Miss Rangaswamy had a portrait in her trunk that Mr. Martin gave to an engraver to copy," Cecilia explained. "We had it printed on flyers, and through the good offices of our servants —including Mr. Charwood—" she said, looking pointedly at Lewis, "they passed out the flyers to house-keepers and butlers. I took one with me to Lady Amblethorpe's Holiday Musicale," Cecilia said.

James leaned back, crossed his legs, and grasped one knee with his hands. "I tell you, Soothcoor, it was the strangest turn of events. It had to be fated that we were there. A woman in attendance said she saw a child with those eyes in her house earlier that day. And to make it more karmic, she told us she knew you as a child and said the boy looked like you," James said.

Soothcoor drew his chin in and frowned. "Who was that?" he asked.

"A Mrs. Montgomery."

Soothcoor stared at him, and if it were possible, Cecilia thought his pale skin grew paler.

"What is it?" Cecilia asked.

He blinked and looked at them as he straightened in his chair. "Yes, I know her," he said gruffly, looking down. "Knew her before she wed Malcolm Mont-gomery." He gave a quick sardonic laugh as he looked up again, his lips twisting. "As children, Lilias, Malcom, and I spent many a summer roaming the Scottish hills of my grandfather's estate together. They were from neighboring families."

"Ah, so not only Sedgewick eyes, but Sedgewick eyes in a child's face," Cecilia said.

He nodded, his lips twisting sardonically at her summation.

"We interviewed Mrs. Montgomery's butler the next day," James said, "and learned the sweep and his climbing boys were at a home up the street. At that home, we discovered Christopher."

Soothcoor laughed and shook his head. And he looked at Cecilia as if much of the stress and worry he'd carried fell off his shoulders.

"You make it sound so easy," Soothcoor said.

James grunted. "That is the short version of events."

"Yes," Lewis agreed. "And while I am exceedingly glad your nephew has been found," he said, "there is more to learn and uncover, especially in light of recent events."

"Ah yes, the matter of Dr. Lakewood. I do not see how he can be involved," said Soothcoor.

A light knocking on the door stopped Lewis from answering. It was Christopher, dressed like a miniature gentleman, accompanied by Miss Rangaswamy, attired in a beige cotton saree with orange banding. She led Christopher over to Soothcoor. Cecilia wondered at Miss Rangaswamy's choice of a saree for her attire. Was it for the Earl's benefit? To stress Christopher's origin?

Interesting. It certainly accented her exotic coloring and appearance. She would have to query her gently later.

"Here he is, my lord," Rani said as she gently guided Christopher toward his uncle.

Soothcoor drew Christopher close. Christopher protested when he would have drawn him onto his lap.

"No, no. I can't see you then." Christopher pointed to the head and neck brace he wore. He could only look straight ahead.

"Ah, does this mean we can play tricks on you behind your back?" Soothcoor asked.

Christopher giggled.

Cecilia did not think she had ever seen 'the Dour Earl' look more at ease. It quite transformed his face.

"Excuse me, madam," Nate said from the doorway. "Breakfast is served."

~

THEY WERE LINGERING over coffee and tea when the

front bell rang. A moment later, Nate escorted the Honorable Charles Sedgewick into the dining room.

"Charlie!" Soothcoor exclaimed as he and the other gentlemen stood up.

Cecilia smiled when she saw Miss Rangaswamy motion to Christopher to stand also.

Soothcoor hugged his younger brother. "Better to-day?" he asked.

"Much and thank you, big brother, for your instance I stop for the night," he said as he avidly looked about the room at the people gathered. "And is this young man in the strange contraption my nephew?"

"It is. Charlie, this is Master Christopher Sedgewick, also known, I understand, as Krishan," Soothcoor said. He turned to Christopher. "Christopher, this is your Uncle Charlie."

"How do you do, sir," Christopher said, extending his hand.

"What? Ah handshake!" exclaimed Charles. "None of that!" He picked up Christopher and gave him a hug before setting him back down. "So, tell me, what would you prefer to be called—Christopher, Krishan, Chris, or something else?"

"Chris?" Christopher asked, his expression twisting his young features.

Cecilia had to keep herself from laughing. His face looked so comical in his serious, considering expression.

Charles nodded. "Yes. Like Charlie for Charles, Chris is short for both Krishan and Christopher."

Christopher looked up at him, his eyes wide, then he turned to Rani. "Would you call me Chris?" he asked hopefully.

She smiled, her eyes misting. "Yes, yes, if that is what you wish, I will do."

"Brother," Charles said, "Who is this delightful, enchanting creature with Master Chris?" he asked, staring at Rani.

Rani blushed and looked down.

"This is Miss Rangaswamy. She brought Christopher—I mean, Chris," he corrected himself, smiling at Christopher, "to England."

Charles bowed over Rani's hand. "Charmed, my dear."

"And this gentleman," Soothcoor continued, pulling his brother's attention from Rani, "is Mr. Lewis Martin from Bow Street. He is responsible for finding Chris."

"Bravo! But I am remiss and seem to have forgotten my manners," Charles said. He turned to Cecilia. "It is a pleasure, as always, to see you, Lady Branstoke. You have been away from London for too long. However," he said consideringly, "for the current crop of debutants, that might have been a good thing. None of them can hold a candle to you."

James rolled his eyes, and Cecilia just smiled. "Enough of the fulsome compliments. Would you like some coffee or something to eat?"

"I ate at an ungodly hour this morning, but coffee would be nice."

She nodded. She looked across the room. "Nate, please have coffee and tea brought to the parlor."

"Yes, my lady."

Rani stood. "I will take Krishan—"

"Chris," Christopher sternly corrected, arms akimbo.

"Chris," she dutifully repeated back.

"I hope I haven't started anything bad!" Charles said.

Rani looked at him. "No, it is fine. I call him Krishan for so long, it will take time to learn again. I will take Chris back to the nursery, as Dr. Seeton is due soon, and he did say only up a short time."

Cecilia agreed and led the others toward the parlor.

The bell rang before she reached the parlor door. It was Dr. Seeton.

While James escorted the others into the parlor, Cecilia escorted Dr. Seeton upstairs.

"Dr. Seeton, a word with you first," she said. "We have another patient for you—perhaps," she said. She led him to her sitting room.

"Perhaps?"

"The patient seems to be recovering, thanks to the good offices of Miss Rangaswamy, though it might be well to have your opinion."

"You have me intrigued."

She gestured for him to take a seat as she sat down on her sofa. "Our maid, Dorothy, accidentally drank some poison last night. Luckily, not much. We got to her before she drank more than a couple of sips."

"You say accidentally…."

"The poison was in a cup of hot chocolate. The intended victim was Miss Rangaswamy, only she does not like chocolate. She told Dorothy she could have it. Dorothy took it to the kitchen to reheat."

"I don't understand. Who would want to kill Miss Rangaswamy?"

Cecilia sighed. She felt her eyes freshening with tears again. She dabbed at them with her handkerchief before answering. "I'm sorry. Just thinking about it again overwhelms me."

"I can well believe that," he said kindly.

She nodded. "Our butler—"

"Your butler?!"

"Yes. He mixed a powder into the chocolate to make her unwell. He says he didn't know what he actually mixed was a poison. Miss Rangaswamy had charcoal amongst her Indian herbal remedies and administered the charcoal to Dorothy."

"For many poisons, if given soon after ingestion, it

is a cure," he said. "Good for her! Yes, I will see Dorothy after I check on Christopher. What was the poison, do you know?"

"Miss Rangaswamy believes it is Kalihari, which is the Indian name for *Gloriosa Superba*. I have learned that, like foxglove, it can be both a medicine and a poison."

"I'm not familiar with that plant. But there is a doctor in London who is familiar with exotic plants and their properties for medicine and poison. You might wish to consult with him."

"Yes! Who is he? Do you have his direction?" Cecilia asked.

"Dr. Jonathan Lakewood. He would be helpful to you. He was one of the lecturers when forensic studies were introduced at the University of Edinburgh."

Cecilia hoped her face did not betray her shock at Dr. Seeton's mention of Dr. Lakewood and his lectures on poisons.

"Thank you for the information," she said. "But I can't keep you any longer. You are here to see Christopher. He is doing much better today. He got up to have breakfast with us, and then Miss Rangaswamy made him go back to bed. They are expecting you."

"Yes. Do you mind if I discuss this further with Miss Rangaswamy?"

"No, not at all. I thought you would want to. My only request is you do not do so in front of Christopher."

"No, certainly not! I understand. Thank you for your candor, Lady Branstoke," Dr. Seeton said as he rose to leave.

"Better to hear from me than through rumors, which so often can take on lives of their own that have no bearing on truth."

"Well said, my lady. Well said."

# CHAPTER EIGHTEEN

"Owen did not like Dr. Lakewood," Damon was saying, when Cecilia entered the library.

The gentlemen rose. "Oh, please, please, sit down," Cecilia said as she walked over to the tea and coffee tray. She made a face. "Bobbing up and down when a lady enters a room or stands looks comical and counterproductive to your discussion. Continue Mr. Partridge."

The gentlemen sat. James looked at her with his enigmatic, slight smile. She winked at him in return, and his smile broadened.

"As I was saying, Owen did not like Dr. Lakewood, and he never trusted Frederick Lakewood. He was suspicious why Frederick was assigned to work with him, and when he tried to talk to his superiors about the younger Lakewood, they brushed him aside," Damon explained.

"But why did he not like Dr. Lakewood?" Soothcoor asked. He sipped his coffee. "I'll grant in my limited acquaintance with the man, I've noted he is dismissive in his manner to those he considers beneath him, but Owen worked with many troublesome people in his life. What was different with Dr. Lakewood?" Sooth-coor asked.

"Brother," Charles said drily, "spend more time in his company and he becomes easy to dislike. I do not like him, either; however, Mama is enamored of him."

Soothcoor raised a brow. "Enamored?"

"Yes, enamored. She thinks he is wonderfully intelligent and wickedly clever."

Lewis's eyes narrowed. "Do you think she would marry him?"

"What are you thinking, Mr. Martin?" James asked. Cecilia sat down next to him, her tea in hand.

"My belief is Dr. Lakewood's interest in Kalihari is profit based. He met Mr. Sedgewick before he went to India, so I assume the doctor was familiar with the severity of his arthritic condition. In India, he saw him much improved. He brings the plant back to England to cultivate and quickly learns it requires a warmer condition than what is typical of England. He needs an orangery or a conservatory," Lewis said.

"He renews his acquaintance with the Dowager Countess of Soothcoor at a horticultural meeting, learns she has the ideal location for his growing Kalihari, and requests permission to plant his specimens in her conservatory."

"I don't think his meeting up with her was accidental," James said.

"You think he learned she had a conservatory and ingratiated himself to her?" Cecilia asked.

"Yes. And I would not be surprised if he has suggested a union between them. Once wed, he gets everything that is hers, which would include the estate with the conservatory and any other properties and money she may have."

"My stepmother is not a stupid woman," Soothcoor

objected. "The only way he would have access to every-thing would be upon her death."

Lewis and James stared at him.

An uncomfortable silence hung in the room.

"You think he would murder her?" Soothcoor fi-nally asked, looking from one man to the other.

"Yes, I do," said Lewis, straightening. "I believe he has decided that this Kalihari plant is his road to wealth and fame. To follow this road, he must get rid of any com-petitors. If he eliminates Owen Sedgewick and Miss Rangaswamy, he is eliminating others with the knowl-edge of the benefits of Kalihari. By eliminating Christo-pher, he achieves two things—any interest the Earl might have in India and this Paradise Medicinals would come to an end, and the Countess would be happy, as you, sir," he said, looking at Charles, "would be the heir."

"Me! I don't want to be the Earl!" Charles protested. "That is too much work and responsibility."

"It is not a matter of what you want, sir, it is what your mother wants."

He looked back at Soothcoor. "He probably thinks to eventually get rid of you, as well, my lord. With the Honorable Charles promoted to Earl, I'm sure he thinks he will have access to more funds, as he will talk you into funding whatever he wants to do as your loving stepfather."

"I ain't no lobcock, to be led around," grumbled Charles.

"Your ramshackle reputation precedes you, Charlie," Soothcoor said. "James, Cecilia, what are your thoughts on Mr. Martin's suspicions?" he asked. "Sounds a bit fantastical to me, but I am beginning to see the ra-tionale."

"When I was above stairs talking to Dr. Seeton, he said there was a doctor in London who was well-versed in exotic plants as medicine and poison. He named Dr. Lakewood. He also said Dr. Lakewood has lectured on poisons at the University of Edinburgh. But we can talk and talk amongst ourselves. However, whom we need to talk with is Lady Soothcoor," Cecilia said. "And find out what Dr. Lakewood has planted in her conservatory, and what are her thoughts and feeling about the man."

"A journey to Richmond," James said.

"Yes."

"I am loath to leave Miss Rangaswamy and Christopher here; however, Christopher should not be in a jostling carriage either."

"I think Mr. Thornbridge and I can remain for protection," Damon offered.

"And I will have some men outside. Today would be a good day, as my informants tell me Dr. Lakewood has a symposium he is engaged to speak at in the city," Lewis said. "I will be hunting him here."

Soothcoor nodded. He looked over at his brother. "Charlie, I think you should stay here as well."

"Why? This is an adventure!" Charles said gaily.

"Which is precisely why you should stay here, as this is not an adventure," Soothcoor said repressively. "Two people are already dead, and someone made an attempt on a third, all because of a plant that Lydia—your mother—may have growing in her conservatory. A dangerous plant, from what we are hearing. You need to discern when your carefree manner is not warranted. I know you can, lest you would not have gotten the high marks at Oxford that you did."

"No one is supposed to know that," Charles mumbled.

"And why is that?"

Charles shrugged.

High marks at Oxford? Cecilia looked at James. He shook his head and faintly shrugged.

"Mr. Sedgewick," she said. "Christopher has had a harrowing experience since coming to England. Your manner is the perfect degree of levity that would do Christopher good right now."

Soothcoor nodded. "Lady Branstoke is correct. Your frivolous and frippery manners would be the perfect nostrum for the child," Soothcoor said, then *soto voce*, "You're near enough the same emotional age."

Charles's mouth kicked up in one corner. "I heard that."

Soothcoor grunted while others held back laughter.

Cecilia rose. "I will need to change into appropriate attire for visiting. I will also see if Miss Rangaswamy has that picture of the plant she said she would draw."

"Yes, that would prove helpful," said James. He looked over at the clock on the mantel. "We should plan to leave at the top of the hour."

"My lord, are you certain you are recovered enough from your journey? You pushed yourself too hard. I believe Dr. Seeton is still here. We could have him check you over."

"That will not be necessary. Sleep was all I needed, and I got that last night."

She smiled. "Good, I am so glad. I will be down again shortly," she said. She turned and left them to their debates and plans.

~

"WHAT DO we say is our reason for accompanying Soothcoor to visit his stepmother?" Cecilia asked as the carriage turned into the lane approaching Eng Appleton, Lady Soothcoor's Richmond estate.

"She is proud of her conservatory. Perhaps you have

an interest in building one on your property?" Soothcoor suggested.

"That is a perfect idea. I believe I have the perfect location for it, too."

"The terrace off the morning room?" James asked.

"Yes. And I can ask if that is a suitable location," Cecilia said.

"I, of course, will be skeptical."

"But you would never say *no* to me," she said coyly.

"Baggage."

She laughed.

"You are well matched," Soothcoor observed.

Was that a faint note of envy Cecilia heard in his voice? She looked at their friend, then back out the window at the manor house as they approached. She would consider what to do about that on another day.

John Coachman pulled the carriage up before the grand entrance to the manor. It was a neat, Palladian-style manor, covered in gleaming white stucco. Connecting at the left side of the building was a large glass and wrought-iron structure.

"An architect would most likely decry the despoiling of the Palladian symmetry with the conservatory addition," James observed.

Soothcoor laughed shortly. "Yes, one tried. The Countess is very good at putting down such affronts and the people who make them."

A footman opened the door as they climbed the front steps to the first-floor entry. Behind him came the butler, crossing the entry hall to them.

"Is my stepmother at home, Jamison?" Soothcoor asked.

The butler bowed stiffly. "Yes, my lord."

"Please tell her I have come to visit and have brought my friends, Sir James and Lady Branstoke."

"Immediately, my lord." He walked toward a door on the left.

Cecilia looked around the hall. It had a grand vaulted ceiling, painted to look like the blue sky, with billowing white clouds. The walls were painted blue, the trim and columns at either end of the gallery style entry were painted bright white.

"The Countess must love the outdoors," Cecilia observed.

"Yes, but like most people with red hair, she burns in the slightest sunlight. When she goes out, she wears the most outlandish large bonnets."

"I am very grateful for my bonnets," said the Countess from the door to the left.

She came toward them. "To what do I owe this visit, Alastair?" she asked, looking from him to the Branstokes and back. "I thought you and Charles had gone to Coor Castle for the holidays."

Alastair brushed her cheek with a kiss. "We had. I rushed back when I learned Owen had sent Christopher to me, but the child had been kidnapped. I came to tell you Christopher has been found. Since Lady Branstoke has been talking of having a conservatory addition to their new estate in Kent and has been questioning me about yours, I invited them to come with me to see yours when I brought you the news about Christopher."

She looked at the Branstokes and smiled graciously. "I am pleased you have an interest in my little passion. Come, let's adjourn to my parlor. It connects to my conservatory, and you will see how beautifully the connection works to bring the wondrous outside into the house. The conservatory extends the width of the house and connects to the dining room as well. Sometimes in the evening I will eat at that end of the conservatory instead of the dining room, if the moon and stars are bright enough."

In the parlor--done in shades of green with foliage wallpaper and floral fabric-covered furniture--the sofa and chairs faced the conservatory, not the fireplace, as was common. Cecilia noted with some amusement that the gown she'd chosen to wear that day matched perfectly with the Countess's décor.

"You have created quite a comfortable room," Cecilia enthused.

Lady Soothcoor smiled. "Thank you. I enjoy it. This is my favorite room in the house. In the spring, the conservatory is a blaze of color. There are some plants blooming there now, ones Jonathan has coaxed to ignore nature's timetable," she said with a laugh.

"Jonathan?" Soothcoor queried.

"Dr. Lakewood, Alastair." She said with a little smile. She rang the bell, and when it was answered, she requested refreshments be brought in.

"Since you came all this way out here, tell me about this boy, for I know you want to. I don't believe he can be Owen's child. Owen swore he would never have a child he could pass his affliction on to, and if he did with an Indian consort, I'm sure he is natural-born," she said repressively.

By her tone and manner Cecilia could well believe that if any would disagree with her, they would find themselves on the losing side. Lady Soothcoor had an elegant, cordial certainty about her that brooked no disagreement.

"Madam," Soothcoor said gently, placing his hand on hers, "I would believe as you, if I had not met the child and spent time with him. There can be no question that he is a Sedgewick, as he has our eyes. You know, we Sedgewicks were often teased as children for our sad, mournful hound eyes.

"Truly, he has your eyes?" she asked, a little worried frown marring her otherwise serene countenance.

He sat back. "Yes."

Jamison entered the parlor with tea and, Cecilia was amused to note, a decanter of some stronger liquid. "Shall I pour, madam?" he asked.

Lady Soothcoor absently nodded, her thoughts elsewhere, Cecilia thought, considering Soothcoor's assertion of Christopher's family resemblance. Cecilia declined refreshments.

Lady Soothcoor looked down as she stirred her tea, then straightened. "Then, of course, we must do right by the child for Owen's sake. We will see that he has an education and is set upon a career path suitable for a natural-born son."

"Lydia," Soothcoor said. "I have heard from several sources that he was married to the Indian woman who is the child's mother."

"And who told you this?" she said, scoffing, "Another Indian? Of course they would say such a thing. Your brothers Langdon and Layton have visited Owen and his *family*, as you call them. Owen has never intimated he was married."

"I am told it was kept a secret because the East India Company frowns on Anglo-Indian marriages, and for the sake of his career, Owen has kept it quiet. He would not tell anyone who works for the company. One person has told me they have seen the marriage lines."

Lady Soothcoor shook her head dismissively. "I'll not believe it. Who told you such taradiddles?"

"Damon Partridge, of Partridge and Sons Imports and Exports."

"Ah, a person in trade," she sneered.

"I do investments with Mr. Partridge. I have never found him to be behind the times in telling truths, even if the truths are hard to hear. But I shall, of course, send to India to see if Owen still lives, and if he has died, as he feared he would, what I can discover about your step-grandson, Christopher."

Cecilia rose from her chair and began to walk about the room, stopping to study the botanic prints on the walls. She heard Lady Soothcoor say tightly. "Charles is your heir."

"A role he does not want," Soothcoor said evenly.

"Nonsense. No one turns aside an earldom."

Cecilia drifted out through the half-open door to the conservatory. She doubted either Soothcoor or his stepmother noted her leaving. She looked back at James. He nodded slightly, as he knew she would look for the Kalihari plant.

The conservatory was beautiful. Sun through the glass all around warmed the space. She breathed in deeply, appreciating the smell of the damp earth and what fragrant flowers that were still in bloom this close to December.

The conservatory was not laid out in neat lines of plants, as might be found in a greenhouse. There was a meandering cobblestone path, crossing first one way, then the other, to give a maximum appreciation of all the plantings. One could forget they were connected to a house.

She walked to one end where a stone bench sat, then turned to walk in the other direction. She didn't hurry. She stopped occasionally to study one plant, then another as she walked. She must be near the dining room, she decided, when she started to see the edible herbs she was familiar with. And she saw the peppers like Miss Rangaswamy had in the box she'd thought was the charcoal. The peppers were bright red. She wondered how hot these were and if Lady Soothcoor ever tasted these or if she just liked growing them. A few feet past the peppers, she finally saw Kalihari, the

Flame Lily. There were three or four plants climbing a trellis, the curls at the ends of the leaves clinging to the supports. One flower bloomed, dark pink, almost purple, with ruffled edges of brilliant yellow. It was easy to see why it was called a Flame Lily, for the petals did resembled flames.

She opened her reticule to pull out the picture Miss Rangaswamy drew for her. She studied the drawing. There could be no mistake. It was identical.

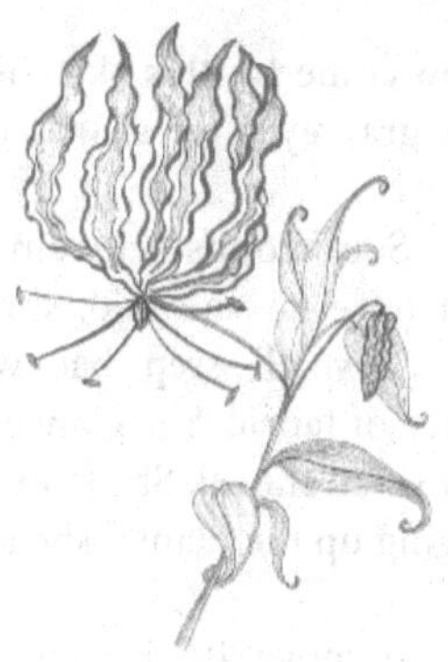

"Beautiful, is it not?"

Cecilia whirled around. *Lakewood!* He was supposed to be in London. And how was it she hadn't heard him enter the conservatory?

She took a step back. "You quite startled me! I thought everyone to be in the parlor," she said. "Yes, it is quite beautiful. And so unusual."

"It is commonly called a Flame Lily, though there is nothing common about this beautiful plant," he said. He reached out to lightly trace the bright-yellow ruffled edge of a rich magenta petal.

Cecilia saw he wore gray leather gloves.

"The proper name is *Gloriosa Superba*, a fitting

name, I would say. But you must know something about this plant already, as I see you are holding a sketch. May I see?" He took the picture from Cecilia's hand before she could draw back. His voice was soft, silky.

Cecilia felt he was playing with her, but she couldn't fathom what he hoped to gain as they stood a mere shout away from the parlor. "It is a good sketch, isn't it?" she said. "I couldn't believe the petals would grow up and away from the plant stamen in quite that way."

"How did you come by this sketch?" he asked, his head canted, his gray eyes ice shards in an otherwise warm room.

"Christopher Soothcoor's nursemaid drew it. I asked if I might have it," she said, shrugging slightly. She took another small step backward. Her foot stepped on a piece of fabric. She glanced down to see a canvas bag and a small shovel. She frowned.

"You are digging up the plant?" she asked. What was he up to?

"Yes, I need to move it." He cut off one of the flowers and stuck it in her hair. "There," he said. "Quite befitting."

Cecilia felt a sudden chill sweep through her body. She thought her blood must have drained down to her toes. She didn't think—from all Miss Rangaswamy had said—that the flower part was poisonous on contact; however, she couldn't help fear from catching at her mind. She understood Dorothy's reaction the previous night.

"This is the plant that provides relief for those who suffer from *arthritis deformans*," he said conversationally as he bent down to pull one of the plants out of the soil.

"Yes, I know. Many plants can provide us with medicines to help. From what I read, we are just beginning to learn the benefits of nature," Cecilia said, striving for as conversational a tone as he.

She watched him pull one of the rhizomes from the plant and use his gloved hand to rub the dirt away.

"Some people have mistaken this rhizome tuber for sweet potato, to disastrous effect," he said. He looked at her. "They died."

"That's very interesting," Cecilia said. "It makes me look around this conservatory with a new consideration. How many other of these beautiful specimens can cause problems for us?" She turned to sweep the conservatory with her gaze as she stepped away.

He grabbed for her wrist, but she twisted away. "No!" she yelled as she ran back the way she came. He chased after her, catching hold of her gown.

"James!" Cecilia screamed. She fell forward into the pepper plants. As she scrambled to get away, her hands grabbed ripe peppers, her fingers digging into the flesh.

"Shut up!" Dr. Lakewood growled, as he hauled her toward him. She was child-sized compared to his height. She struggled and kicked against him as he brought the rhizome to her lips.

She clenched her teeth, swinging her head from side to side. She got a hand free from where he'd caught it between her body and his and pushed against his face. She pushed her bare fingers across his eyes. The juice from the peppers she'd crushed in her fingers touched his eyes. He howled in rage and pain and released her.

Then James was there, tackling Dr. Lakewood. They fell into one of the planting beds, crushing the luxuriant green foliage, dirt spilling into the cobbled walkway.

Soothcoor grabbed Cecilia by her shoulders. "Are you all right?"

All she could do was nod.

"Jonathan!" wailed Lady Soothcoor.

Soothcoor pulled a small knife from his pocket. He grabbed Lakewood by his coat where he rolled on the floor, fighting to get away from James. He pressed the knife against his neck.

"Stop. Ye twitch again and I'm afraid the knife will cull ye," he ground out.

Lakewood, his eye red and watering, looked sideways at Soothcoor. He let go of James.

"You have it wrong! I stopped her! She was going to steal the *Gloriosa Superba* plants," Dr. Lakewood protested. He looked over at Lady Soothcoor.

"Lydia!" he cried out.

Lady Soothcoor looked from Dr. Lakewood to the Earl.

"Alastair! What is going on?" asked Lady Soothcoor. "Jonathan! Why did you attack Lady Branstoke?" She looked around the ravaged beds with broken and uprooted plants and loose dirt strewn across her neat cobblestone walkways.

"That woman was going to steal the *Gloriosa Superba* plants. She has a sketch so she would know which ones to take. I couldn't let her do that," Dr. Lakewood babbled.

Soothcoor dragged Lakewood to his feet, while James untied his cravat and wrapped it around Lakewood's wrists, securing them behind his back. Soothcoor grabbed his upper arm and turned him about.

"Don't let them do this!" Lakewood pleaded over his shoulder to Lady Soothcoor.

"And I was not believing you could be guilty. A man o' medicine." Soothcoor shook his head as he pushed Lakewood toward the dining room.

James gathered Cecilia in his arms. She rested her face against his chest as her heart slowed its rapid drumming.

~

"I LET MY GUARD DOWN," Cecilia said an hour later, as she, James, and Soothcoor sat in the parlor with Lady Soothcoor.

The local magistrate had reluctantly taken charge of Dr. Lakewood, and messages had been sent to Mr. Martin.

Cecilia had washed her hands several times to remove all traces of the hot pepper on her fingers and scrubbed her mouth to remove any bits of the *Gloriosa Superba* plant Lakewood had ground against her teeth, trying to force-feed her the poison.

Her dress was horribly stained. The second gown she'd ruined in as many days. She'd liked the dress. She had been considering having a matching pelisse fashioned for her, one on which she could add some bits of embroidery. There would be other dresses and pelisses.

"I should have been paying better attention to my surroundings," she said as she sipped a small glass of sherry.

"None of us expected him to be here," James said. He looked over at Lady Soothcoor. "Is that true for you as well, my lady?"

"Yes. He said he would be in the city all day, that he had a lecture to give this afternoon."

"I wonder what caused him to come here to steal the Kalihari away?"

"I'm certain Mr. Martin will get it from him. However, if I were to guess, it would be the climbing boy coming to us when Peasey died," suggested James.

"Why would that matter?" Cecilia asked. "People die every day in London under some of the worse circumstances. It's unfortunate, but a fact of life in the city."

"And why Mr. Thornbridge wants to leave the city behind," said James.

"Yes," Cecilia acknowledged.

"The climbing boy knew Peasey's wasn't a natural death. He went for help to Daniel, and Daniel knew to bring him to Mr. Martin or us. I believe Lakewood was nearby when Peasey died. He probably wanted to learn more about how the poison worked. And remember, Daniel said the other day he'd seen the gray man in the area coming and going," James explained.

"When the boys came to us, Lakewood probably realized we would investigate and not take that death as any death in London. And later, there was no excitement around our house as there might be if someone— like Miss Rangaswamy— died of poison. He knew something of his plan had gone wrong."

"But what was his plan?" Soothcoor asked.

"To make medicine using the Kalihari plant. To treat people with the plant. For a profit. Sufferers like Owen and their families would pay any amount to have their suffering eased, especially during our cold, damp English winters."

Cecilia nodded, thinking through James's summation. "I am also wondering if there wasn't some ego involved as well. He had a reputation of knowing poisons. With the medicine solution, he could lecture on the two aspects of many plants—poison and medicine, and how to work with a potentially lethal substance and bring it to a successful resolution."

"He would have a reputation for broad knowledge and would be asked to lecture. When someone gets notoriety, they are in higher demand in their industry and can get higher lecture fees," Soothcoor suggested.

"Owen willingly let him have samples of the Kalihari plant," Cecilia said.

"But he didn't give him any samples of the medicine derived from the plant. Kalihari is a dangerous plant to experiment with. This frustrated Lakewood. He didn't want to take years to learn what a sample might tell him," James said.

"We should return to London," Cecilia said, as she set her sherry glass down on the table beside her. She frowned and picked up an ornate, oval-shaped silver box she saw sitting next to her glass.

James saw what was in her hand. He raised an eyebrow as they exchanged glances.

"Lady Soothcoor," Cecilia said as she stared at the box sitting on her palm. "May I ask where you got this?"

"Dr. Lakewood gave it to me, but it doesn't work." She looked at Soothcoor. "You always enjoyed tinkering with things like this. Perhaps you can get it to work."

Soothcoor frowned. He reached out a hand to take the box. "It looks like the Singing Bird box Owen had from his mother."

"Oh, my," Cecilia said, "I feel like bouncing up and down as Miss Rangaswamy would. If Dr. Lakewood had this, then this is likely the same box!"

Soothcoor looked over at her. "It was the only item missing from their luggage stored in the Waddley warehouse.," she explained. "Miss Rangaswamy said it was Christopher's favorite item, even though it was broken, and he slept with it every night."

"If I can get it open, we can know for sure if it is the same music box. I worked on it years ago for Owen."

"My lord! You never cease to amaze me," Cecilia said.

He smiled a crooked smile at her as he reached into a pocket in his waistcoat and pulled out a leather pouch. From inside, he extracted a small screwdriver. "Let's see if I can't get this fixed right now. Having his silver box back—and working—should make Christopher happy."

They watched Soothcoor delicately remove the tiny screws from the bottom of the box. He removed the plate the screws held in place. He stared down at the mechanism.

"What is it, Alastair?" Lady Soothcoor asked.

He set the screwdriver and plate down on the table next to him, then reached into the box. He pulled out a tightly folded piece of paper.

James laughed. "I think I know what that paper is."

Soothcoor nodded. He unfolded the paper and held it up.

It was the marriage certificate of Owen Sedgewick and Sushmita Dhar.

Lady Soothcoor gasped.

He leaned back in his chair. "Owen put this in the music box to make sure I got it. He knew I would fix a broken music box. He must have suspected someone would try to destroy evidence of his marriage."

"When Miss Rangaswamy told us Christopher's broken music box was missing from the luggage, she did say Owen told Christopher that his uncle would fix it," Cecilia said. "I didn't realize she meant that literally." She looked over at Lady Soothcoor. The woman had tears in her eyes.

"My lady, I'd like you to return to London with us. You cannot want to stay here alone tonight."

Lady Soothcoor looked down at her hands, then back up at Cecilia. "Yes, I think I should like that. I should like to meet my new step-grandson."

Lord Soothcoor rose from his chair and went to Lady Soothcoor. She stood up and Soothcoor enfolded her in a hug. "Thank you," he whispered.

James passed Cecilia his handkerchief. Cecilia gave a watery laugh as she blotted her eyes.

# EPILOGUE

## MARCH 1816, SUMMERWORTH
## PARK, KENT

*C*ecilia stared at the knotted mess she had made. She was sitting in their morning parlor, enjoying the sunshine streaming through the window. Outside, a hint of green tinged the trees and peeped up through the dirt, promising spring. She was looking forward to late spring, with everything in bloom.

Her neighbor and friend, Lady Elinor Aldrich, had been teaching her to tat. As Cecilia stared at her wayward knots that did not follow the prescribed pattern, she feared tatting would be another of the female skills that would elude her. She should stick with embroidery. At least when she made a mistake in her embroidery, she could carefully pick the threads out. It wasn't so easy to do so with tatted knots. But the tatted end result was so pretty—if one knew what they were doing. Since there were paper patterns, Cecilia thought it would be easy to learn. It had not turned out to be so! She wondered if that was because her mind slipped its leash and wandered too much when she sat still in one place. She had to pay close attention to what she was doing with tatting—more than she was wont to give.

Perhaps she could get the bad knots out—but on another day when her frustration was not already high.

"Cecilia!" She heard James call for her. "Cecilia! We have received the most amazing communication from Soothcoor," he said, as he walked into the morning room, laughing.

Cecilia set her sewing basket on the floor beside her as James crossed the room to sit beside her. He drew her into the circle of his arms, giving her a squeeze and a kiss on her brow.

She snuggled against him. "Don't keep me in suspense. What is happening in London?"

"Do you remember the climbing boy, Billy?"

"Yes. I remember two things best. He had a delightful cheeky smile when he was happy, and then, the horror of his relating Mr. Peasey's death."

"Mr. Martin got him into a school for boys."

"A school we pay for," Cecilia said.

James inclined his head. "However, he is not there now."

"Oh, please don't tell me he has run away!" Cecilia said.

"On the contrary. He was a model student."

"Then what happened? Where is he?"

"Soothcoor adopted him."

Cecilia's eyes grew round, and a broad smile lit her face. She clapped her hands. "How delightful! So he will be a big brother to Krishan," she said.

James shook his head and laughed. "Not quite."

Cecilia frowned. "You are deliberately toying with me. Please tell me what is going on."

"This past Sunday, they read the banns for the first time for the marriage of the Honorable Charles Sedgewick and Miss Rani Rangaswamy."

"I would not have thought —" Cecilia's thoughts

swirled. "How delightful!" She clapped her hands together.

"In four weeks, they will marry at the same church where we were married, and later that week will board a ship—with Christopher—to sail to India."

"Why are they going to India? I know Soothcoor has received word of Owen's death."

"They are going to settle Owen's estate. I'm told the house and its contents are valuable. Langdon and Layton have had a difficult time keeping others from assuming ownership. Charles, going in the official capacity of Soothcoor's agent, can settle Owen's affairs. Owen did well for himself and Soothcoor wants to make sure Christopher's inheritance from his father is intact. And, though he doesn't say so directly, I believe they will see if they can make Paradise Medicinals a reality."

Cecilia nodded. "I'm glad Miss Rangaswamy has found her path. She is a joyous young woman."

"Yes, she is. Though I remember at one time you considering her as a match for Mr. Thornbridge or Mr. Martin," he teased.

She laughed. "I did. I like them all, and I want all of them to have happiness."

"They will find their way, my love."

"I know, but—"

He laid his finger across her lips. "Hush. We have plans to make in our own lives without making plans for others," he said, as he gently laid a hand on her stomach.

Cecilia laid her hand over his. "Yes, we do. No more wishing for another mystery," she said.

"No mysteries? But we have one now. Will our child be a boy or a girl?"

She laughed. "Yes. And that is mystery enough," she admitted.

James nodded. He loved Cecilia's laugh and loved making her laugh.

She slid her eyes up to look at him, a small smile playing on her lips. "At least for the next few months."

James scowled at her, then laughed. "I'll take however long a reprieve I can get."

## The End

Gentleman's Trade

Reckless Hearts

A Lady Follows

The Rocking Horse (novella)

Perchance to Dream (short story)

# ABOUT THE AUTHOR

I live in Florida, seven miles from the Gulf Coast, with Ken and our six cats. I decided to be a writer when I was in the fifth grade. I filled notebooks with stories—until a mean-spirited high school teacher told me I had no talent for writing. Crushed, for several years I stopped writing, but writing was an itch that wouldn't go away.

My interest in the Regency period came while in high school when I volunteered to re-shelve returned books at the community library. Every week there were Georgette Heyer novels to be shelved. I finally checked one out and became immersed in the world of the Regency.

Fast forward ten years. When attending Science Fiction Conventions, I met people who read science fiction, but also enjoyed the works of Jane Austen and Georgette Heyer, just as I did! They liked these books so much that they wore Regency costumes at the science fiction conventions. They even had Regency era dancing on the convention program. These science fiction readers and writers knew a lot about the Regency era. Intrigued, I did research on the era and quickly went from casual Regency reader to a Regency history buff. Woo-hoo!

After that, with encouragement from science fiction authors, it was just a small step to writing Regencies.

Subscribe to my newsletter to learn about books and other writings I'm working on. You can sign up here.

## Or visit my website